INDEFINITE
DETENTION

KAM R. JOHNSON

INDEFINITE DENTENTION
A novella

Copyright © 2022 by Kam R. Johnson
All rights reserved.

ISBN:
978-0578280370
Library of Congress Number:
202290600

Cover art by:
Anastassia Johnson

"From my Soul to Yours."

Contents

ONE

Honk, honk! The bus horn rudely woke Heath up. Then he heard his mom yelling "Heath, get up! The bus is here early!"

Heath sat up quickly looking at the clock and it was only 6:15 a.m. Even his golden lab dog Scooter laying on the floor beside his bed looked sleepily up at him with a seemingly disgusted look on his face. He was named Scooter because when a puppy he would scoot along the floor to get to you.

"Alright! Have him stand by!" he yelled back. Heath scrambled for his clothes that he luckily had set out the night before. "Cripe's sake he's early! Arghhh this really stinks!" he grumbled to himself. "Scooter, where is my shirt?" He looked quickly around and realized Scooter had taken it off the chair and was using it as a pillow. "Sccooooteerrr!!! Give me that!" He pulled the shirt away quickly so he wouldn't have to play tug a war with him.

Heath quickly put on his clothes, patted Scooter on his head, and ran into the bathroom. He brushed his hair and glanced at the toilet wishing he had time to use it. Honk, Honk! "Alright, alright, I'm coming!" He then bolted for the front door being held open by his stepdad and who also had yelled to the bus driver that Heath was coming.

He nodded to his stepdad who shrugged his shoulders and said, " I hope they have breakfast for you!" He always got up early to care for the many chickens they had.

Heath suddenly heard his mom from behind, "Good luck son, I love you!"

He turned and kept walking backward as he waved back at her as she stood in her bathrobe in the doorway. He could tell by her voice she was getting emotional. He quickly turned then and ran forward. He didn't hear her tearfully talk to his stepdad as he hugged her with his one and only arm. He lost the other in a recent farm accident.

"What will happen if he fails school? What if we can't pay our bills soon?" she asked out loud as she watched her son move forward into the early morning darkness. She watched him with a heavy but hopeful heart.

It was a typical very warm and muggy north Florida July morning, with darkness and heat lightning flashing in the distance. Heath lightly jogged down the dirt driveway with many pecan trees scattered on both sides. A rooster was crowing and he could smell the chicken manure. At 17, he was 6' tall, strong, and lean with light brown hair. He had been told he was handsome, and generally was a quiet thoughtful teenager. He was also sporting a fading left black eye. Heath easily hopped over the driveway gate and stood before the open door of the yellow school bus. Summer High School was displayed in black letters along its side. Its reflective markings and flashing lights contrasted with the dark and rain-drizzled morning. It was a clean small yellow bus, and the driver was a silver-haired man perhaps in his late sixties, looking impatiently but kindly at him.

"Come in quickly please sir, I have other pickups to get" he said as he smiled with a clean-shaven face. The driver was in typical senior clothes, but his demeanor and cleanliness reminded him of a high-powered executive type he'd seen on TV. He had a perfect silver haired haircut, perfect teeth, and was wearing an old expensive looking gold watch that he kept glancing at and then back at Heath as to give him a hint. He wore faded tan khakis and a plain long-sleeved gray button-down shirt. You could tell he was tall and in great shape. Heath grabbed the rail and stepped cautiously up one step and looked into the back of the bus before going further. He could see a long black arm laid out sideways against the back corner of the bus. Also, two long black hairy chicken legs hung over the seat in front of the hidden body with giant big foot size high-top sneakers on the feet. Loud snoring could be heard from the bus's only other current passenger. Getting a better look at the face, Heath let out an involuntary snicker.

"Ha! Let me guess, Jeeter!"

The bus driver with one arm on the door handle trying to close it with Heath still in the way, said in his distinguished butler voice, "Yes sir."

Heath got on and walked towards the back as the bus lurched forward. After shaking the snoring passenger's leg, Jeeter sleepily awoke.

Jeeter smirked and exclaimed loudly, "Heath bar!!" He then demanded a high five from Heath and stated "Jeeter's the name, and summer school is the game!"

Heath smiled and shook his head back and forth. "At least I'll have good company!"

"Oh yeah!" Jeeter said giving a thumbs up, as he laid back and closed his eyes, "pop a squat bro!"

The bus picked up speed as it had turned onto a paved road. He stayed standing holding onto a seat and looked towards Jeeter thoughtfully. He hadn't seen him in several years. His locker had been next to his in 8th grade when they'd first met. Even back then Jeeter was 6'3" tall and very skinny. In gym class, Heath had never laughed so hard when he saw Jeeter doing jumping jacks. He looked like a giant scarecrow flapping his arms! Jeeter had a very laid-back disposition and enjoyed the outdoors like Heath. They had become good friends for a while, even though they had ended up in different high schools because of their school's zoning boundaries. They managed to fish together a couple of times during eighth grade and the summer after. They had talked about girls and their future. They had planned on going into the military, mostly because both of their families could not afford to help them with a car, college, etc. The economy was slow, even for hard-working families like his own. You couldn't even sell out a farm to retire, nobody was buying. Heath sadly reflected because of his stupid misdemeanor mistake, the military probably wouldn't even take him, even if he managed to pass summer school and graduate next year. Heath laid back in the seat and gloomily looked out the small bus window. He wondered how many other failed students they would be picking up. The darkness and rain reflected his mood. The last few years had been a bumpy ride for him. If it wasn't for his love for his mother, and even his dog Scooter, he had almost just run away. Hopefully, travel across the world and be free! Work a little, play a little.... No school, no responsibility, no worries. He relaxed further back in the seat and closed his eyes. He could hear the rain and Jeeter snoring loudly again. The bus hummed along and soon he fell asleep also.

Heath awoke abruptly to the sound of a loud voice cussing. It was broad daylight he observed and the bus was traveling down a winding bumpy dirt road, splashing through large mud puddles. Nothing but trees, cows, and pastures could be seen everywhere. As he sleepily looked around on the bus, he noticed Jeeter had also just awakened in the back and was looking forward. Towards the front, a short heavy-set teenager was leaning back in the seat with his fingers in his ears. He also noticed the bus driver had a tough and rough-looking teenager standing next to him. The rough boy had on a short sleeve t-shirt and a cigarette pack in the front pocket. He also wore faded jeans and some old sneakers. There was a dragon tattoo on his upper muscled left arm. He looked taller than Heath but shorter than Jeeter. His hair was black, combed, and lengthy. Heath immediately pegged him as a large bully type with a chip on his shoulder. The kind Heath hated but knew in a fight they both would lose some teeth. He looked familiar to Heath. He was pretty sure he had seen him working with a mechanic in a local garage one time.

"What the #$!! do you mean you had made a wrong turn? Where in the $%#@ are we?" he loudly asked. "Can you believe this guy?" he yelled as he glanced at us in the back. The rough/tough-looking teenager was holding on to the back of the bus driver's seat with his left hand, and waving an unlit cigarette angrily around with his right hand while shaking his head. "Un freaking believable!" he shouted.

Jeeter sat down next to Heath while still half asleep. "Yea, where are we is right?" he said looking around out the window.

Even so, we've been driving a long time, and I have no idea where we're at!"

Jeeter smirked, "Maybe we'll have school with the cows today. We get there when we get there," he said as he was crossing his long arms and leaned back in the seat while yawning. "So long as we get credit for a school day!"

"Ha-ha, same old easy-going Jeeter. Don't you ever get mad or upset?

"Heck no", Jeeter answered closing his eyes. "I go with the flow and stay cool. Getting mad takes too much energy!"

"That guy standing next to the bus driver must be burning a lot of energy then!" Heath thought out loud. He glanced around and then looked over at the heavy-set boy again, who was sitting towards the front left. The boy looked at least a year younger than Heath. He had pale skin, short reddish hair, and looked like a bookworm. Wonder why he has to go to summer school? Heath pondered to himself. The boy had on new expensive-looking clothes and was staring out the window avoiding eye contact. First impressions made Heath think he rarely went outside and did nothing physical." What's your name buddy?" Heath politely asked.

"Ron"...the boy said turning slightly red, then quickly faced out the window. Heath figured Ron was not only shy but was nervous about Heath's black eye. Heath suddenly felt his ears pop like they had been traveling northward. He hadn't felt that happen since the first and only time he went up in an airplane. He opened a window next to him to let fresh air in. His mouth tasted funny, and he felt groggy like you would after dental surgery. He needed to pee bad, and he was getting sick of the loud complaining and yelling the big guy was giving the bus driver. He couldn't blame him much though; this was getting ridiculous. How could a bus driver get lost? In 1983, there were no cell phones, only pay phones, and gas stations to ask for directions. Heath looked towards the bus driver and the noise. He was ready to complain also but saw the big guy was doing enough for all of them.

He heard the bus driver say, "Almost there, almost there" in a calm voice.

The large boy yelled back. "Eat my shorts! You have us in the middle of nowhere pops!" yelled the muscled teenager.

Heath stared at the big guy, noticing he was sweating and getting angrier. He kept touching his cigarette pocket with one hand while waving the other angrily in the air. Glancing outside again he observed them passing another heavy-looking gate, and we're going more and more uphill. Cripes, was this a school bus or a tour bus? He thought to himself.

"Finally!", he heard the big loudmouth say as he watched him point towards the front of the bus in the distance.

It was weird Heath thought, that he was in such a hurry to get to summer school? At that, all stood up in the moving bus while they held onto a seat in front of them. The big-mouthed teenager was already standing next to the bus driver. The chewed-up paved road turned into a long rugged dirt driveway of sorts, lined with trees. There were a lot of bumps from small holes. As the bus pulled into the large dirt circle driveway, it stopped in a dust cloud in front of the small school.

When the bus door opened, Heath sped out past the big guy who had sat back down and quickly headed for the backside of a nearby tree. The heavy kid slowly followed Jeeter out and both started stretching themselves outside.

When Heath returned saying "Ahhhhhhhh much better", he stood by Jeeter staring at the school.

Ron continued towards the small school entrance on a pathway. He was enthralled by the delightful smells of cooked breakfast emitting from the open door. An American flag flew in front of the new-looking cement block building. A large professional-looking sign over the door indicated "Summer High School."

"Guess it's new" Jeeter stated glancing behind him, and noticing the big guy had gone to the back of the bus and sat down.

Looks like what's his face is quitting early to take a nap!"Heath smirked, following Jeeter's gaze behind him.

"How did you get that black eye anyway"? asked Jeeter.

"Awwww a schoolmate and his friends were ragging on my garage sale clothes, and we got into it. I've had some detentions, some unwanted fights, and bad grades. I try to make extra money with after-school jobs instead of studying sometimes. Guess that's why I failed my last year."

"Ha-ha... man, what a goober!" Jeeter said smiling.

"How about you boys get in there? Better eat your welcome breakfast before it's all gone!" stated the bus driver who had gotten out of the bus, and stared stretching as they had.

Heath and Jeeter complied and walked suspiciously forward. While doing so Heath asked, "Don't you think this all weird? Where are all the other buses?"

"Jeeter replied," I'm sure we're last, but let's watch pork boy eat first. If he starts foaming at the mouth like a sprayed roach, we are outta here!" Both laughed and walked into the school.

As the distinguished bus driver continued stretching outside, he casually watched the boys go into the school and observed behind him that the larger teenager had sat back down in the back of the bus. He then got back onto the bus near the driver's seat and fiddled with some clothing and stuff jammed on the left side of the seat's floor, all the while looking towards the teenager in the back. "Aren't you going to get some breakfast inside? You don't want to be late your first day!"

The large teenager was still sitting, and angrily looking through the bag he had brought, as well as his cigarette pack. He apparently was frustrated at not finding something and was sweating hard... perhaps not just from looking frantically. "Go away and mind your bees wax pops!" he demanded.

The bus driver stood up tall and walked slowly towards the angry young man, his hands behind his back in butler fashion. As he got within five feet of the teenager he stopped. Calmly he said, "You won't find it sir"

The large teenager froze, and then he slowly stood up beside his seat while glaring at the bus driver, his face sweaty and furious. Both were tall and strong, but the bus driver was nearly fifty years hi

The bus driver calmly replied back

Most people looking at the large muscled teenager's reaction at that point would have been backing up and preparing for escape or battle. However, the bus driver's face and clear steel-blue eyes just calmly looked back.

Angrily the teenager yelled, "You destroyed my stuff?!! When I was sleeping?!! Have you got a death wish? Are you freaking crazy!?" The large teenager slowly stepped toward the bus driver a couple of feet closer. "I don't care who you are, or how old you are, you are getting a beating for that!!!" The huge teenager, old enough to join the military, lifted up his fists furiously and slowly started for the old man!

The bus driver stayed where he was, and replied calmly, "You have the whole world figured out, don't you son? No mystery, no dreams, no hope for the future?" Fifty thousand volts and a quarter of an amp came out of the taser guns' several wires, hitting the angry teenager in the chest, almost the same time his fist was flying. The bus driver was standing at an angle, his right hand holding the taser which had been hidden behind his back. He continued to depress the taser's trigger, as the teenager's body stood upright, stiffly and shaken for several seconds until he fell to his knees. The bus driver calmly stepped around to the back of the teenager, keeping the trigger depressed. He then dropped the gun, and then quickly fished out some handcuffs. He then expertly handcuffed the large teenager's hands behind his back, as if he had done it for years.

"Sorry son, you left me no choice. You will be tired for a day, but no permanent injury........"

Two

As Heath and Jeeter walked into the school, both noticed four large comfortable-looking school desks of sorts in a line to the left of the large room. The chairs faced towards the right wall, which had a long-looking light bar of some kind across the top. The same wall with a high ceiling also had some small recessed gadget-looking devices, speakers, and stuff it looked like. Both smelled the freshly cooked food from across them, in covered trays from a closed-type kitchen opening in front of them, on a countertop.

Ron was sitting at one of the desks and was humming a happy tune while eating a large tray of food. "Doo doo doo, doo doo doo" he was singing to himself. It looked like eggs, bacon, juice, and chock-let milk and donuts he was eating. Heath's stomach was growling but stayed where he was and continued to stare suspiciously around the room.

Jeeter after looking around started for the food, commenting "Well, he is still alive!" he chuckled. MMMMMM, I'm starving!"Heath followed and both grabbed trays of food and sat with Ron, each on a large desk. Soft 80's pop music was playing in the background. Jeeter dove into the food, but Heath just nibbled and pondered aloud.

"Where is everyone? Why are there only four chairs? This is weird I tell you!"

Ron was in heaven eating his donut and said nothing.

Jeeter looked up, "Maybe this is a new modern type school? Maybe there are other groups in other areas? Maybe we are the special ones!" Jeeter said smiling gulping down his food.

At that moment big Shawn looking sweaty and exhausted suddenly stumbled into the room from the back hallway area. He fell to his knees and had his hands handcuffed behind him. No one noticed until just then that the main door had shut, and clicked with a heavy lock. The music had also stopped. All froze with fear....

"Guess we are special" Jeeter whispered and gulped loudly....

A handcuff key dropped to the cement floor from Shawn's big hands behind him. "They tasered me...gave me a shot in arm.... need my, my, bag"....he stammered in exhaustion. After he breathed in deeply, he yelled "UN cuff me you pinheads!!!" Shawn yelled.

Ron, red-faced and shaken, backed slowly up against the wall his face in fear.

Heath's temper kicked in and he started kicking and crashing his body against the heavy steel front door hollering "Let us out!!!"" Let us out!!!" His adrenalin kicked in, and after failing to damage the door with his body, he attempted to grab a desk to hit it with, but the desks were bolted to the floor!

Jeeter, his face with fear and concern watched Heath's failed attempts.

Shawn grabbed his attention suddenly. "I'm going to hurl! Shawn said gagging with nausea.

Jeeter, noticing the handcuff key on the floor, grabbed it up and clumsily managed to remove the handcuffs off Shawn's wrists. Shawn struggled up on his own and stumbled around the back corner where he had entered from. Loud puking could be heard from him in that area. Heath and Jeeter followed, and saw big Shawn knee-led down in a big bathroom in front of a toilet, puking his guts out. Heath and Jeeter saw another side steel door, just past the bathroom's entrance on the left. Both started kicking it to no avail.

"We're trapped! What the #@!! is going on here!" Jeeter yelled, looking at his friend.

As Jeeter and Heath went around kicking, yelling, cussing, and Shawn puking loudly, Ron put fingers in his ears, closed his eyes, and slumped to the floor like a sack of soft potatoes. Time had seemed to slow down for all of them......total fear of being obviously imprisoned, and coupled with the long trip and adrenalin burnout after several minutes, it suddenly became quiet. Shawn staggered back out to join them looking pale, sweaty, and weak. He was wiping his mouth with his hand. He smelled of sweat and puke. He grabbed a glass of water off the caged kitchen counter of sorts and drank some. Heath and Jeeter were burned out also and just looked around at each other in shaken disbelief and exhaustion. Suddenly all eyes were on Ron in the corner, he was pointing upward behind all of them. As they all looked behind them at the large tall wall with the long display across the whole top, it was flashing words.

"Welcome to Indefinite Detention. No harm will come to you. Repeat. No Harm will come to you. All will be explained in time. All please be seated." The same sentence rolled repeatedly across the display... For the first time, all four looked at each other repeatedly and continuously with darting eyes. All hoping this was a joke or a bad dream.

With the combination of exhaustion, and hope for answers, all four slowly picked a desk and shakily sat down. The words "No harm will come to you" displayed above, definitely gave them temporary courage. The desks were very comfortable and of high quality. The surface area was large and thick. The desks were about two feet apart and had comfortable armrests. Several minutes of deep breaths passed by before Shawn spoke."

Some nurse gave me a shot in the arm". When the other three looked at him, Shawn was looking intently at his left arm. He was pale and shaky but didn't appear to be nauseous anymore.

Jeeter noticed first you could adjust the seat on the desk to push it back. He stretched out his long legs. The desk he noticed also was attached to the floor, with large bolts in cement. I guess we would be dead by now if that's what they wanted...." Jeeter blurted out nervously.

Ron again noticed the changed message being displayed, and pointed towards it, causing the others to take notice. As all read it, panic and fear froze them in terror!

The message displayed in bright red letters with no sound.... "You will not be harmed. All will stay here for a while...together. You will all be cared for. You will all be released to return home, only after completing classes of school subjects and discussions. The faster the completion, the faster all will return home...." The message continued repeatedly as all four stared unbelieving, trying to make sense of it. Wondering if they were being punished, or in some sick experiment? But by who? So many questions.... Some clicking noise was heard from behind, and all flinched hard. A steel door behind them had opened slightly. All stood up defensively and instinctively, side by side, ready to face any threat best they could. When nothing happened, Shawn slowly went forward and peeked behind the slightly opened door. He threw the door wide open, and all noticed four large bunk beds, a shelf of books and games, two large closets, and even a laundry room. Nobody entered the room.

"Is this for real "Ron whispered loudly in total fear..."

"This is bull@#%!" shouted Shawn, suddenly turning to face the other way. "I know we are being watched!! I'm not playing your sick game! Let us out of here!!!" he roared. The others felt the same way. All were in denial. Ron accidentally got too close to Shawn and suddenly got shoved hard by Shawn. "You trying to kiss me!?" Shawn yelled. Ron went flying sideways and crashed against one of the bolted-down desks and fell. He slowly stood up in obvious pain.

"It was an accident!!" Ron yelled back red-faced and tearful."

Jeeter pointed at Shawn and yelled, "That's not cool dude. We are all in this together!"

Heath watched closely and had guessed what would happen next, and so as Shawn dove for Jeeter's neck with two large hands, Heath dove for Shawn's midsection in a tackle. It felt like hitting against a huge tough punching bag. As all three were in a tangled mess wrestling and cussing each other, Heath and Jeeter against big Shawn, a loud hissing noise was heard by all. From all directions, a cloud of foggy mist filled the large room. The noise alone stopped the fight, but then all felt sleepy.... so sleepy.

When all four slowly started to wake, they had no idea the time. No windows were in the building it seemed. Heath noticed first the large display, it indicated a time of 1715hrs, and continued with the words "No harm will come to you." Shawn staggered towards the bathroom gagging again. Jeeter sat up groggily, and after looking towards Heath, he noticed the display also. Ron also got up from the corner rubbing his face and shaking in fear. He headed towards the bathroom and waited his turn. Getting all the way up, Heath and Jeeter stretched and rubbed sore body parts from the wrestling. Luckily the fight was a wrestling match, Shawn had apparently elected to keep it that way. No lethal punches or kicks had been thrown, but of course, the apparent sleeping gas had made it short. Jeeter noticed cups of water on the kitchen counter area that was mostly caged shut. As he drank some he noticed Heath was looking at the paper and short blunt pencils on each desk. After all had drunk some water in suspicion and rotated bathroom use, the display changed and all sat down reluctantly. The display in large red letters scrolled across the top...."No Harm Will Come To You... Please follow these rules to shorten your Indefinite Detention. No swearing, no fighting, treat each other with respect, stay clean, obey instructions, do assigned chores, complete all assigned tasks, participate in future discussions.....more to follow."

As the message repeated itself, Jeeter looked at Heath next to him and asked" So we will have a teacher? For discussions?"

Heath shrugged his shoulders and fiddled with the

paper on his desk. He breathed a slow deep breath trying to calm himself, and mumbled "This is so crazy....who would do this!?"

At the desk on one end, Shawn jumped up and swiped his paper to the floor, yelling "Screw you all and your rules!" Ron sitting beside him flinched hard and leaned in his desk away from him. Shawn now standing, was doing a hand crank, making his middle finger slowly go up in his left hand, as he turned his right hand in a cranking motion. He looked around the room in angry defiance. Jeeter watching couldn't help a snicker. The display changed again...."All must work together.... all will pass and go home together...or all will fail together, and stay here Indefinitely. Now write a letter to your family saying you are all ok and you want to explore the world for a while, also say you will stay in touch by mail, and not to worry."Heath, Jeeter, and Ron digested this mentally while fiddling with the paper and pencil.

Shawn continued standing, his paper on the floor, and smiling evilly as he continued to flip off possible watchers around the room. He kept repeating" screw you...screw you...screw you!"

Watching, Heath suddenly lost his temper again. "We all feel the same way but we can't escape, and we will just get gassed again! So let's just play their stupid game for now!"

Shawn looked hard at Heath. He pondered to himself thinking should I slap that kid silly, or is he making sense? He felt terrible. He had a headache, his mouth was dry, and he felt weak. He knew he was having drug with drawls. He also suddenly realized the shots someone had given him were probably helping him. After taking a deep breath and to everyone's surprise, he picked up his paper and sat down. I'll play along, for now.... Shawn thought to himself. All four tiredly began writing to their family as instructed. They wrote how they wanted to explore for a while and that they would contact them occasionally to let them know they were all right. Ironically, unbeknown to each other, they each acknowledged to themselves that the thought had actually occurred to them for real. As teenagers there were so many unknowns, so many decisions, so many requirements, and constraints, and yet would they ever see their family again? One by one each finished while having a thoughtful and fearful look on their face. The most fearful being Ron, the least fearful in appearance being Shawn. Instructions continued from making a clothing list of sizes, preferences, food allergy notices, and overall health concerns. When done, all papers were directed through the kitchen opening. When completed the display indicated a supper time soon to follow, and that class would start tomorrow morning at 0900hrs after breakfast. A supper of heated frozen dinners soon ensued. Other side dishes of various snacks fruits and rolls were included. Drinks included milk, water, and cool-aid. Heath and Jeeter noticed Shawn and Ron ate like there was no tomorrow.

"Where do they put it all?" Jeeter whispered to Heath.

"I hear you idiots talking, mind your own business!" Shawn snarled, as he wolfed down a fruit cocktail in one hand and chewed on a roll with the other. Ron was almost keeping pace, wolfing down a third container of pudding.

When all four were finished and hurting from eating too much, more instructions were displayed...."All will dispose of dishes and trash through the kitchen entrance. All desks will be wiped down with cleaners in the bedroom closet. All will help and all will obey instructions. Again, failure to do so will result in bland food, sleeping gas, and or delayed progress of your return home!"

Heath, Jeeter, and Ron started to comply right away, while Shawn stayed in his chair and burped. After a few minutes of watching, Shawn reluctantly got up and shoved his dishes in the kitchen slot. He then headed to the bathroom around the corner. Soon the shower could be heard running. After cleaning the other three did a slow search of their apparent prison. In the bedroom area were extra pillows, blankets, soaps, and even four electric razors. Nobody was in the mood to look at the books or games. Each sat down on a bunk, waiting their turn for the bathroom.

A sudden yell from Shawn made all three jump with their hearts in their throats. After a cautious look around, the three crept up to the closed bathroom door.

"Turn the shower back on!" yelled Shawn from within.

"Nobody is touching it!" yelled Heath towards the door.

Jeeter turned and walked back towards the bedroom mumbling; it's going to be a loonggg night!"

The display caught Ron's quick eyes again and said "Look!" Heath and Jeeter looked and couldn't help a snicker. The display read "The shower has a three-minute time limit for each person, once a day, period." Shawn was still yelling....

When all had showered they eventually migrated to putting on clean underwear and robes provided in their room. As Shawn did a slow search around the inside of the building apparently looking for escape points, Heath and Jeeter chucked everyone's dirty clothes into the washing machine. Ron sat on his bunk, red-faced and scared in thought. Noises could be heard in the kitchen area, obviously, someone was using a dishwasher. A steady muffled noise of a big generator could be heard somewhere outside in the backyard. Soft pop music began to play from somewhere, and Heath and Jeeter speculated to each other why this was happening.

"They obviously are doing some kind of experiment. If they wanted us dead or something else, it would have happened already" Heath said out loud.

Jeeter laid back on his bunk in thought. "Yes, I agree," Jeeter replied sighing. "But why us!?"

Heath laid back on his bunk also and remained

silent. He hoped his mom and stepdad wouldn't worry too much. He wondered if the police would be called? How would they find them? He didn't even know what county, or even what state they were in? The drive here was obviously many hours long. He suspected now some type of sleeping gas was used in the bus as well.

Jeeter stretched out his long legs and groaned. He glanced toward Ron. "Hey bro, can you pop the clothes in the dryer when done? I may pass out soon. Hopefully, we will all wake up alive!" As he snickered to that out loud bravely, inwardly he was scared. His parents divorced recently, and so his mom had to get a job. As she was gone a lot, he had skipped school frequently to play basketball by himself at the park. His dream was to play professionally starting in college, but between lack of money, bad grades, and the yelling of his parents, he wasn't even able to play in high school. Truth be told, he had no idea what he was going to do with his life, and now this! During the night, they all tossed and turned in the room. They all had fallen asleep but soon after, all awoke to the sound of a helicopter taking off and leaving from close by. Periodically they all had a turn in the bathroom during the night. Night light plug-ins were in some of the room's electrical outlets. Afterward a quick wander around the dark building, then back to tossing and turning. A ceiling fan and vented air coming thru the ceiling vents helped with airflow. Ron snored so bad, that Heath woke up and threw his pillow at him. During the night also, Shawn cut the cheese long and loud, causing Jeeter to throw his pillow at him in disgust.

"Barf me out!!" he whispered to himself. Shawn just sat up, took the extra pillow, and went back to sleep.... Ron later on also cut the cheese loudly in his sleep. Jeeter pulled his robe over his face and turned toward the wall. "It could gag a maggot! These people are disgusting!"

THREE

The sound of a radio announcer talking about the weather slowly woke everyone up. Its sound increased until all were awake. Having no windows like prison was disorienting. After a minute of stretching, yawning, and scratching, Shawn got up first. He was in a foul mood. "You losers better help me when I figure out to get the @#! % out of here!" he hissed angrily. Turning he grabbed his clothes out of the dryer and went out left towards the bathroom. The other three got up also while the radio increased in noise coming thru the speakers in the large classroom area. They too grabbed their clothes and sleepily put them on. Dread and anxiety-filled all their hearts.

Jeeter however bravely exclaimed, " We are still alive! No butts, no guts, no coconuts!" Health forced a smile at Jeeter, giving him a knuckle touch. Ron still sleepy struggled with putting on his pants. Heath, Jeeter, and Shawn had old faded jeans, while Ron had new name-brand tan khakis. Falling to the ground on his back like a turtle, Ron stayed there and struggled to pull his pants over his soft fat stomach.

Jeeter couldn't resist a comment...." Bro, do a sit-up once in a while, and maybe eat less". Ron ignored him and turned away his red face. Jeeter continued, "I mean no offense."

Health, smelling coffee and eggs through the door opening, gently pushed his friend forward curious to see.

As they entered the main room, they could see the display showing 06/15/83, 0730 hrs. Many high school students in the early eighties had bought digital watches, a new fad. So military time was somewhat known. Fads of smoking, Nike sneakers, MTV, boom boxes, video arcades, Rubik's Cube, and roller skating were in also. Heath did or had none of those things, except a Casio digital watch he had bought himself. He also loved his clock radio, record player, and cassette player he had at home. He would record his favorite songs when they came on the radio. As he grabbed some food and coffee from the kitchen opening, he was suddenly homesick. He felt like he was in a weird dream, but he knew he wanted to survive whatever this was and get home soon.

Soon all four were heartily eating scrambled eggs off paper plates and drinking milk, juice, and coffee in paper cups. Afterward, Ron tattled off to the bathroom, when all heard him suddenly yelling "Gross!"

Shawn still eating started laughing out loud. "I left

you all a present of grand scale! My best work yet! Ha Ha!" As Shawn laid back in his chair grinning evilly, Heath and Jeeter carefully went to see.

Ron was practically gagging at the bathroom entrance and pointing to the toilet. "I can't go with that there!" he yelled louder than he'd ever spoken before. Jeeter and Heath noticing the very large and long human waste plugging the toilet quickly pinched their noses and ran out.

Jeeter being Jeeter, couldn't help a snicker while still plugging his nose. "You have to admit, that is probably world record-breaking!"

Health didn't have his sense of humor and could feel his temper rising. He looked hard at Shawn. "You expect us the clean that up!?"

Shawn calmly looked at Heath from his chair. "No dipstick, I expect the prison guards to clean it up, or they will have to let us out!"

For a moment that got Heath thinking of possibilities, but then Ron increased his yelling saying "I have to go bad!"

Also, Jeeter noticed first, that the display had changed. It read "A plunger and cleaning supplies are in the hall closet. The class will not start until cleaned. All delays will increase your detention here. Your destiny is in all your hands."

Shawn sat up suddenly cursing, and Ron's yelling got louder. Jeeter stood beside Heath, both yelling at Shawn to clean it up! Pushing and shoving ensued; it began to look like a real fight would start. At that moment though very loud sirens and horn-blasting noises started. The lights also started flashing and a message of: "One week added to your indefinite detention" was displayed. As all covered their ears it finally stopped after an agonizing full minute.

Eventually, all retrieved the plunger, bleach, mop, and paper towels and got the job done. Shawn pretty much just handed over the cleaning items to the rest while Ron motivated to use the toilet very quickly did the worst parts. He stuffed paper up his nose and came close to puking several times. After bagging up the trash, and all washing their hands at least three times each, Ron yelled "Get out now!!" He pulled his pants down the second the door closed. As he did his business the other three went into the main room. On the kitchen counter were four stacks of school books, Indefinite Detention had begun!

Over the course of many weeks, they all slowly got into the tiresome and dreaded routine. At first, all were given easy intro school books on American history, English, Maths, Science, and Biology. It was a go at your own pace. Tests in the book were open book and had to be ripped off and entered into the kitchen slot upon completion. Periodic messages, noise punishment, plain food, no desserts, and even skipped meals helped keep them in check. Ron began to hoard snacks in his room when they came available, which the others thought was a good idea. Ron always finished his work first and then headed to the room for his snack hoard and book reading. Heath and Jeeter would compete with each other and be about even. When done they would play board games or write more letters to home indicating they were alright. Shawn would instead pace the building, or do push-ups in the classroom area. Shawn was always last with the bookwork and would be routinely embarrassed and frustrated with himself and the situation. Many of the message threats of having to stay longer, or noise punishment, stemmed from his swearing or bad attitude. However, with do-overs, corrections, and late-day work, Shawn managed to keep up.

One morning they all woke up with many packages in the main room. Each person received new jeans, shorts, shirts, socks, underwear, and even new tennis shoes, according to the size they had described earlier. All were good quality.

"Well, whatever this prison bull crap is they seem to try to meet our needs," Heath remarked.

Shawn quickly growled out loud. "Yea, but that cuts no ice! We are not mice you SOBs!" He then did his usual middle finger up while slowly turning around, daring anybody that was watching to stop him. Ron quickly stuck his fingers in his ears and fell accidentally in fear of noise punishment, but they lucked out. Shawn looked disgustedly down at Ron, "Smooth move ex-lax!"

It wasn't until all had eaten breakfast and were

putting their new clothes away in the large bedroom area that they all heard a new voice.

"Class has started, please be seated!"

All four teenagers froze in shock. The voice coming from the large classroom area was a female one! It was also musical sounding and reverberated clearly in the next room. Shawn was the first to slowly walk out through the bedroom door and looked in astonishment! The others crowded close behind him. A very pretty woman in a tight but conservative red dress stood calmly on the right side of the room, under the display bar facing them. She was tall and had long blonde hair and blue eyes. She looked around thirty years old. Other than blinking normally with a slight head movement she stood militarily. All four moved quietly and sat in their large comfortable desk chairs, their books neatly stashed underneath on a metal shelf. All stared hard at the woman in anticipation and amazement!

"Thank you," she said, looking at each of them. "Please just call me teacher. We will have daily discussions on various topics. Participation is mandatory. There is no right or wrong answer, just an exploration of ideas and thoughts." She paused to let that sink in and then continued in her musical female voice. "Nothing has changed. You all will be here until completion. All self-guiding bookwork will continue when I'm not here. You all will have to pass together, or none will go home. I suggest all of you lower your egos and ask for help from each other when needed. I will not answer any questions, but you all must answer mine."

Heath looked at her in astonishment. He couldn't help but ask what was on everyone's minds. "At least tell us why we are here?" he asked.

She stared at him a moment at perfect military attention and replied. "Upon completion, you all will be advised. The harder you work the sooner that will be." Turning her head to face them all and smiling showing perfect white teeth she said, "Let's get started then! Let's talk about leadership. There are as many methods of leadership as there are people in the world; I would imagine anyway. Leadership is defined as, the position or office of a leader. Most people would probably say also, that it's a person in charge, or in power. Heath, describe how a leader should lead?"

Heath still looking at every detail of the seemingly perfect physical teacher, quickly sat up in thought and embarrassment. "I guess a leader should be fair and reasonable," he said." The teacher continued to look at him. Heath continued after a short pause." The leader should also care a lot about the people."

The teacher smiled greatly and nodded her head. "I would say that's the most important, and then all else would follow. "How about your thoughts Jeeter?"

Jeeter was relaxed, slouching in his chair with his long legs extended out and crossed. Jeeter stretched out and yawned putting his hands behind his head. After eating always made him sleepy. "I think a leader should be smooth and cool. He should be dressed with style, and wink at all the ladies!" he said with a smile.

The others couldn't help but crack up, before the teacher quickly asked, "Can a leader be a woman? Or someone older or younger than you? Or someone with a disability? What do you think Ron?"

Ron blushed beet red and looked down. After a long moment, he managed "Sure."

The teacher realizing that's all she would get and moved on to Shawn. She looked at him and asked, "And you sir?"

Shawn breathed out slowly and loudly as if he would rather be catching rattlesnakes instead of being here. However, he answered. "A leader needs to be strong and not a sissy. He needs to know what the @%! & he or she is doing! I also would not take any orders from a kid! I don't care how smart the kid is. A leader has to be respected!"

The teacher nodded her head." I appreciate all your thoughts. As we know from history or even your own experiences, there are of course good and bad leaders. A leader/parent/boss etc. can improve or destroy a family, a business, a city, or even a nation. A leader can effect changes small and large and may have ripple effects for a lifetime, or even generations. A leader can inspire good-will and love toward each other, with freedom and exploration, or a leader can inspire fear, hate, suffering, and just plain evil, living only for his or herself and not putting the people first."

Shawn suddenly stood up. "Ha!" Pointing a finger at the teacher he yelled," and what kind of leader are you?! As we are prisoners!" Heath, Ron, and Jeeter also fired up by Shawn stood up also angrily and glared at the teacher. To everyone's surprise, the teacher took a step forward and glared back at all of them.

"Make no mistake, right or wrong, our objectives with you all will be fulfilled! Your length of stay will be determined by your participation in all discussions, your compliant behavior, and all four of you completing and passing all bookwork!" After a minute of all staring at each other, the teacher's intense face relaxed, and she backed up a step. "I'm sorry, but you all are in Indefinite Detention, and its duration is up to you all!"

After another minute one by one the teenage captives silently sat down, all with a reoccurring feeling of dread in the pit of their stomachs. The teacher sensing their feelings said, "Pay attention a little more and you will all be rewarded with a gift." At that statement, all sat up with curiosity.

She continued," People even thousands of years ago had the same problems, fears, questions, and hopes as we all do now. They also had good leaders and bad leaders. Some had kings or governments. Learn from the decisions and actions of past leaders. For example, Proverbs from the Holy Bible describes without wise leadership a nation falls. Also, Plato, a Greek philosopher in ancient Greece hundreds of years ago, wrote that a leader should be a lover of wisdom and have the moral strength for the common good. Have fairness, restraint, and courage. Lastly, lead by example! If a President or parent drank heavily, did drugs, cussed obnoxiously, dressed sloppily, etc.. would that not be embarrassing to the country, employees, or child? If the leader wasted money but raised your taxes, is that not hypocritical? If a parent does not discipline the child reasonably for bad behavior, regardless of how much it hurts the parent, would that not create an unruly spoiled child that most likely would end up in trouble later in life?"

"Jeeter! Conclude briefly what was discussed."

Jeeter, taken by surprise lazily sat up. He calmly took a deep breath and sighed loudly before slowly answering as he gave thought. " Uhhhhh, I guess a leader should be caring,.... uhhhh not hypocritical.... Clean.... and lead by example.... no matter how much it hurts," he said the last smiling.

"Good job!", the teacher said also smiling. "You may all now go outside!"

You could almost hear all four of them stop breathing and gulp at the same time at the words, "Go outside!" They all looked at each other in wonder, and then at the teacher in disbelief. The teacher calmly smiled and pointed towards the back hallway leading past the bathroom. A loud click was suddenly heard, echoing in the back hallway. As if on cue all four stood up cautiously, and proceeded excitedly in that direction. Shawn led, getting to the heavy side door first. It was slightly open letting sunlight and fresh air in. Shawn pushed the handle, opened the door, and walked through with the others close behind. All had to squint and shade their eyes with their hands. The sun was bright, the air fresh, and a slight warm breeze brushed across their smiling faces.

FOUR

quick survey by all revealed they were in a large prison-type exercise yard. The large area was enclosed by an obvious electrified heavy mesh fence, topped with sharp razor wire. Three large rows of razor wire were also across up high across the building itself, an obvious deterrent to prevent roof access. The whole exercise yard was attached to the far left of the main building and was greatly recessed, so had not been seen from the far right entrance of the school/ prison. A half basketball court was on one end, and a boxing ring on the other far end. Dumbbells and a heavy bag were next to it. Next to the doorway and slightly undercover was a large waterproof bag of basketballs, hats, sunglasses, suntan lotion, bug spray, and even punching gloves. Jeeter and Heath quickly grabbed two basketballs.

"Nice!" Jeeter exclaimed. Music suddenly came on outside speakers.

As Jeeter dribbled away, and Ron slowly walked around, Shawn grabbed some boxing gloves and stared hard at Heath.

Looking back at Shawn and at the boxing gloves Heath said "No thanks."

Shawn frustrated, hissed "No you idiot, our future way out!" he said jerking his head towards the fence.

Heath then started dribbling the basketball and quietly replied," We need planning. We are still being watched." Heath then headed towards Jeeter who was happily making shots.

"Let's play 21 bro! Jeeter hollered.

Shawn was pumped up. He eagerly put the gloves on and started hitting the punching bag. He instinctively felt this would be the best area to escape from. Glancing around, he carefully noticed everything in detail. He noticed how very high the fence was, how small the mesh was, the large rolls of razor wire, and the radical curve at the top. He couldn't help but admire the design and expense behind it all. As he punched away he began to feel better and more himself. Starting to do drugs as he had was very stupid he realized now. He missed working his muscles and feeling invincible.... this was his true self he realized.

As the music played the happy voices of Heath and Jeeter bantering each other while playing basketball were heard. Ron slowly walked around enjoying the outside also. He felt lonely and sad for himself. Eating so much all the time and coupled with being shy had made him an invisible person in school. He was very unhealthy and even now breathed hard from just walking. He observed Shawn happily hitting the heavy bag, looking so powerful and seemingly indomitable. As he walked around slowly his keen eye glassed eyes observed the outside speakers, cameras, and high-tech display bar. He was astonished at its futuristic ability. Even in his high-tech magazine subscriptions, such as Popular Mechanics, etc., he had never seen the like. Whoever has imprisoned them was obviously many decades ahead of the times and had a lot of money. His thoughts were suddenly interrupted.

"Hey Ron, catch!" Heath seeing Ron wandering by himself felt sorry for him. Ron on the other side turned towards him, his face blushing a deep red. Heath gently as he could threw the basketball towards Ron, using a powerful underhand throw. The ball bounced in front of Ron's slow response and banged against the back fence causing a spark from the shock before it rolled away close to Shawn.

"Throw it back!" Jeeter yelled out encouragingly to him.

Ron, feeling the pressure of the others staring at him walked over and picked up the ball. Shawn standing close by took an interest and faced Shawn smirking in anticipation.

"Throw it hard jelly belly!" Shawn hollered close by.

Ron still blushing and nervous leaned back with the ball in both hands and threw it hard as he could towards Heath and Jeeter at the other end. Instead, the ball drove downward and connected perfectly between Shawn's legs who was only a few feet away.

"Awwwwwwhhhrrgggh!!" Shawn howled in pain, dropped to his knees, and covered his private area with both hands, howling like a dying beast! Ron quickly ran towards the school back door entrance in terror, praying it was still open as he was gasping for breath. He quickly ran into the building and locked himself in the bathroom. Heath on the other hand was laying down outside and laughing so hard he was crying.

Jeeter was cringing with his fist in his mouth, "Dude, that's got to hurt!"

Shawn's eye was watering and he bent over on his knees still dealing with the pain. "Ahhhhowwww, stupid jelly belly" he mumbled to himself half aloud. After several moments he forced himself to stand up and angrily looked hard towards Heath and Jeeter still visibly laughing. Heath much more than Jeeter.

"Oh-oh" Jeeter said looking towards the very angry Shawn. Heath still laughing had stood up, and followed Jeeter's gaze towards Shawn's angry face who was now walking towards them. The outside bell was about to ring to bring them inside, but it wasn't necessary. Both Heath and Jeeter ran towards the back door with the charging bear Shawn roaring behind them!

"Gangway!" Heath yelled as he and Jeeter scrambled

inside against each other as they entered and fought inside trying to pull the door in, but Shawn was grabbing the outside door knob and was pulling hard also. A Hard tug of war ensued, while Heath and Jeeter on the inside were hollering "Calm down!"

Big Shawn on the outside had a foot planted against the wall of the building, and replied "Screw you!" Shawn slowly gained distance against the other two, and as one knowing each other well, Heath and Jeeter let go at the same time! All three fell backward in opposite directions. Heath and Jeeter crashed against the inside hallway wall behind them. Shawn with no wall behind him flew backward further away, and much harder! The door closed automatically to the relief of the three inside. Shawn, with his now bleeding-skinned hands and a sore behind, quickly got back up and pounded on the door while cussing for all he was worth.

Lunch was served inside and after clean-up, the message indicated "Back to bookwork." As they worked it was hard to study. All three inside worried what Shawn was going to do when allowed back in! After the meal and an hour of bookwork, the outside door could be heard automatically unlocking. Big angry Shawn walked in behind the other three surprisingly fast after the click of the door. The other three looked up at the sweaty and injured beast and prayed the sleeping gas was going to kick in. When it didn't, Ron looked pale and slowly moved towards the wall in hopes of running around him for the bathroom. Heath and Jeeter huddled up and backed up preparing for battle. The quiet and heavy breathing from all seemed ominous. Shawn, taken aback at the fear and concern on all their faces from his presence suddenly felt satisfied. In fact, he actually started to chuckle. Then he full-out belly laughed! The other three shocked at this felt relief. Seeing and hearing Shawn laugh so hard, something they had never seen before, started laughing also. They all laughed so hard it was hard to breathe. Shawn still laughing and shaking his head grabbed some water and a cold sandwich. He then sat down. It was going to be OK.

The following day encompassed a quiet morning of breakfast and slow bookwork. The pattern continued of Ron finishing first, who then cautiously helped cranky Shawn, and then either Heath or Jeeter afterward. Nobody could progress too far unless all had caught up. The bookwork was submitted in sections only. Papers then would be submitted thru the kitchen counter slit, and would again be corrected and returned at various times. Failure caused all to halt until returned papers had to be looked over and redone. Nobody ever saw a hand or movement when the papers were returned. Noises could be heard at various times behind the counter, especially around meal times. Unknown to the teenagers, the real summer school bus had come to each of their houses, about twenty minutes after on the morning day of their kidnapping. After that first school day calls were made to the four teenagers' homes from the real school. When they didn't see them that night, all parents, except for

Shawn's dad who didn't keep track of Shawn anyway, searched their known hangouts and then finally went to the police department. Information and pictures were given out to all surrounding areas, as a BOLO. Even when the letters from the teenagers arrived days later it was suspicious. No fingerprints other than the missing teenagers were found on the letters and all were post-marked locally. Even as the search expanded they had no idea the teenagers weren't even in the state of Florida at that time.

After eating lunch consisting of Sloppy Joes for food, Capri Sun for drinks, and an hour of outside time, all returned to their seats. The teacher stood in tall straight military fashion, already waiting for them. She wore a similar conservative dress as before, but today it was blue. Her hands were folded behind her back. All four of the boys pondered her entry and exit methods to the room. All had never-ending questions to themselves.

"Let's begin with a fun question for all of you." The teacher slowly turned her head looking at each of them in turn. Her eyes were bright and shockingly clear, and her musical voice was unusual, to say the least. "Tell me, if you could be an animal, what would you be? Also, why that choice? Ponder that for a moment. Remember, take my questions seriously, but know that there is no wrong answer." At the request, Ron on one end began turning red and was doing his usual squirming in his chair in anticipation of talking out loud. Jeeter next to him leaned back and placed his hands behind his head and yawned loudly. After having breakfast, lunch, and basketball, he was ready for a nap. Heath next to him leaned forward in deep thought of the question. Shawn on the other end was relaxed in thought also. However, his hands were unclasped, and he was looking intently at the teacher.

"Mr. Ron! Your answer please sir?"

Ron, red-faced quickly turned his face away to the right away from sight, and mumbled softly, "a pig I guess."

The Teacher and the others looked at him, "I'm sorry, say again louder please?"

"I said, I like to eat a lot, so I guess I'm a pig!" Ron shouted still facing away, his arms now crossed.

Silence filled the room until a snicker from Jeter's cupped mouth snuck by. Then Heath and Shawn couldn't help their loud laughter either and let it loose hard. The pressure was too much, even though they also had tried to cover their smirks with their hands as Jeter had tried. Shawn was laughing so hard that he had a hard time breathing. Ron sank into his chair.

The teacher crossed her arms and tapped her foot angrily. "I guess outdoor privileges aren't important anymore!" the teacher yelled out. Quiet came quickly, even though Shawn, Jeter, and Heath had to clamp their hands across their mouths again very hard to accomplish it. The teacher shook her head. "I'll say this again, we are all friends here."

At that, Shawn let out a loud snort like a bull, crossed

his arms, and again stared intently at the teacher. The teacher glanced at him but continued.

"Your turn Jeeter."

Sitting up, and still trying to stop himself from trying to laugh, Jeeter replied. "I'd like to be a panther maybe, just chill and take cat naps in the sun."

The teacher nodded and looked at Heath. Heath responded, "I guess I'd like to be an eagle or a stallion in open country. I'd run free and explore, take a break from stress and people.

The teacher responded with a smile, "Very thoughtful."

Jeeter next to Heath reached and gave him a knuckle touch." Gnarly, way to go Mr. studly! Heath chuckled at that with him.

The teacher then looked at Shawn and quietly awaited his answer. Shawn looked intense and stood up as if to stretch. His slow delayed response and movement caused all to look curiously. Shawn suddenly grinned evilly.

" Why I guess I'm a lone wolf, always have been. Yes, a big bad wolf!" His speed surprised all as he leaped forward around the back of the teacher, and put his arm around her neck! He squeezed, and his arm went thru her neck!! He fell back in shock and horror!

Heath and Jeeter stood up and practically fell backward over their chairs. Jeeter yelled in total fear as he hurt himself banging against the bolted-down desk." She is a freaking ghost!!!" Shawn, Heath, and Jeeter all slammed backward against the wall, in fear and confusion, trying to make sense of it all! All were trembling and panting heavily in shock. Their mouths were dry. As they stared at the teacher in her calm military fashion, only Ron seemed suddenly unafraid. In fact, to the amazement of the others, Ron with his mouth in astonishment and breathing heavily walked forwards to the teacher and stuck his arm through her body! He then waved it back and forth as it passed thru its body.

The teacher looked down at him and smiled, "you understand now, don't you my intelligent friend?"

Ron smiled in great wonder. "You are a Hologram. Amazing!" he whispered loudly. Long minutes passed before all got their calm back. Ron in his choppy and shy way quietly pointed out the tiny pieces of equipment from the ceiling, which projected the Hologram and gave it movement. Unheard of in 1983, except in science fiction movies. Ron very briefly explained his knowledge of its possibility from popular mechanics magazines. Whoever was responsible for all this, was very very ahead of the times! Eventually, all four sat back down and faced the teacher/hologram. All students were still in awe.

"Well, now that we got that out of the way let's close with some thoughts. I think you all can agree now never assume that everything you see is real. Television for example can use tricks, lies, and illusions, as well as crooks, military in war, politicians, and even law enforcement. Try to expect the unexpected; open your mind to think outside the box. These things can be used for good or evil. Never judge a book by its cover. However, looking at Ron, A brain needs a healthy body, to sustain and protect it. Additionally, looking at Shawn on the other end, A healthy body needs a healthy developed brain, to also sustain and protect it as well. Agreed?" Surprisingly, even though shaken from the surprise of the hologram, all nodded their heads in grudging respect of these truths. "Class dismissed". For the first time in their presence the hologram then abruptly disappeared, again totally freaking out all of them.

That night in their bunks all the boys were still astonished and shocked from the day's events. All were tired and were close to asleep when Heath couldn't help himself.

"Hey, Shawn. You awake?" Heath whispered loudly in Shawn's direction in the dark.

Shawn's body was seen turning on his back in the dim light. "What is it?" he grumbled sleepily."

Heath whispered "I was just curious. Were you going to choke that teacher out? If she was real, I mean"? Jeeter and Ron became more alert in the dark at the question. Ron pulled his covers up and thought it wasn't wise to poke a sleepy angry bear. However, all eagerly awaited his response.

Shawn was heard to let out a slow frustrated breath. "Listen closely dork heads. I am not a stinking killer. I was just going to choke her a little until they let us out. I was going to use her as a hostage until we go out of here!! Cripes!" He said angrily. "How could I know it was a freaking hoolagram, hologram, whatever it is!" Shawn laid back down.

"OK OK, don't have a cow!" Heath replied. Heath, Jeeter, and Ron however did feel better and fell asleep faster.... knowing his answer.

One late afternoon weekend, Heath was singing in the bathroom during his three-minute shower. Jeeter paused in the hallway near the closed bathroom door to sing along. It was "Come sail Away" by Styx, written by Dennis DeYoung. Heath and Jeeter sang it loud and proud. "I'm sailing away, set an open course for the virgin sea. I've got to be free, free to face the life that's ahead of me. On board I'm a captain, so climb aboard. We'll search for tomorrow, on every shore. And I'll try oh Lord, I'll try to carry on!" They sang it pretty well, and cat napping Shawn awoke and listened with interest. Ron however had to pee badly, and since the side door was unlocked on weekends, he went outside to pee.

"Awwwwwwwwwwohhhhhh!!!!"

Jeeter quickly ran outside to see what was going on. He then saw Ron on the ground holding his groin area with both hands. His face was grim-icing. Looking at the evidence, Jeeter exclaimed. " Duuuuuuude bro! You never pee on an electric fence!"

Perhaps due to the fascination with the technology and shock of the hologram, several weeks went by without issues. They continued to plow along through the many discussions and hours of bookwork. As always, the book reviews in the back of the books and corrections submitted back to them helped them to progress. Additionally, the encyclopedia books, geography books, American History books, etc. in their room assisted also. Their education level was greatly improving. Being in Indefinite Detention with little distractions and freedom as a goal, was a huge motivator. Every day, however, they each dreamed of completion, escape, or home. One morning for whatever reason they were told discussion would start after breakfast instead of in the afternoon, and then it would be an early day off for them. Most of the time their schedule was routine, but occasionally it changed. The change in routine seemed to correlate with a helicopter coming or going.

The day began with soft background music and a healthy breakfast. Overall, they enjoyed a variety of food. Routinely, Shawn would jump ahead of the others and grab the food he wanted first from the side kitchen opening in the wall. "Snooze you lose! Suckers!" he said grinning and daring anybody to challenge him. Ron would be drooling close behind him. Heath couldn't understand the rush as obviously they weren't going anywhere. Then after the routine of cleanup and bathroom breaks, class started with them saying the daily Pledge of Allegiance. A waving American flag would appear in hologram style, and even Shawn stood with his hand on his heart.

"I pledge allegiance to the flag of the United States of America, and to the Republic for which it stands, one nation, under God, indivisible, with liberty and justice for all."

As the four sat down to hopefully get the lesson over with soon, Jeeter started up his daily humor and teasing.

"Hey Ron bro, I couldn't help notice your boner gave you trouble sitting down! That hologram turning you on huh?" Heath exploded in laughter, and Ron took it as usual with no comment while turning beet red. Shawn snorted loudly and burped out his breakfast while leaning back with his hands behind his head.

The hologram materialized and immediately began scolding in its female musical voice. "I was going to say good morning gentleman, but I see you boys are no gentlemen. Humor is great, as long as there is a willing participant and not at the expense of another!"

Jeeter replied, "Shucks I was just kidding. Glancing at Ron he said "No hard feelings bro". Ron just stared forward and crossed his arms.

"Today let's give thoughts and talk to the bigger questions of life. Where did we come from? Why are you here? What is our purpose? Why do we humans have self-awareness, and free will, and are given control of this planet?" The teacher hologram switched it up and looked directly at Shawn first. "How about it sir?"

Shawn rolled his eyes expertly, and stayed leaning back as he indicated he could care less." We are told always in school that something blew up, some soup was made, and abracadabra, millions of years later we evolved from monkeys. Then, here we are!" he then waved one of arms around in the air indicating everything. The teacher continued to look at him in silence wanting more. Shawn sighed loudly. "I believe as they say it's survival of the fittest. The physically weak will not evolve and then die. The end."

The teacher was impressed. "Very good Shawn. You put it in a nutshell what public schools teach their students." Shawn looked back at her with a dazed, when will this end look.

"Your thoughts, Heath?"

Looking uncomfortable but determined, Heath then replied. "I don't believe that!", he exclaimed suddenly." I grew up Christian."

The teacher noticing his hesitation gave him support." Well, considering America's laws come from Christian values, our money has printed" In God We Trust" on it, our pledge of allegiance says "One Nation Under God" in it, and our military is buried with a cross, I'd say millions of people worldwide past, present and future will agree with you, Heath."

Looking down in thought Heath took his time before continuing. "I don't believe the whale, the eagle, a rainbow, the fish, and humans were just slapped together accidentally from an explosion. Life is too perfect, too complicated, and diverse. Our self-awareness is no accident!"

A few moments of quiet filled the room. The other boys appeared somewhat surprised at his clear and determined response, and they glanced at him with curiosity. Heath actually surprised himself.

The Teacher looking at Heath challenged his determination. "So, Heath, you don't believe time changed dinosaurs into birds, monkeys into humans? You don't believe your great, great, great, great, grandfather was a rock or a dot in space?" The boys all laughed at the latter, relieving some unexpected tension in the room.

Heath smiled, "No, I do not."

The teacher then turned her head. How about you Mr. Jeeter?"

Jeeter was somewhat taken aback by the serious nature of the discussion, and how deep Heath's thoughts were. His own serious thoughts on the matter were usually passive and uncaring in behavior.

"Honestly, I never really gave it serious thought. I believe we have a choice for our destiny. My family is very laid back and we don't talk about that stuff. We are just chill I guess."

The Teacher then seemed to gather her thoughts for a moment. "Please know I'm not judging, or worthy of being a judge. I'm only making you all think of a bigger picture than just existing. You can believe you came from a rock, or that you were planned for, and perfectly created with a free will, by God, the creator of everything. I think most all agree that self-awareness, internal knowledge of right and wrong, human emotion, the balance, diversity, color, and variety of life, did not come from an exploding dot in space."

The teacher continue,. "As we all know, there is love, sacrifice, forgiveness, and truth that "creates" the existence of good families, bonds relationships, gives purpose and encourages knowledge. Societies, Countries, etc. that build on all that also, will thrive and prosper. On the flip side, hate, evil, selfishness, lies, and unforgiving, can destroy the existence of self-esteem, purpose, and relationships. It affects individuals, knowingly, or unknowingly. It can destroy Nations. Now also, look at being "neutral", not picking a side, or involving yourself in anything. Just survive for yourself only." The teacher looked directly at Shawn now. "Does being selfish belong in the good or evil category? Does being self-absorbed do anything? Does this incredible existence of possibilities and free will, have any value in being neutral? Is then being neutral, a total waste of its astonishing one-of-a-kind creation?"

An electric and dramatic silence filled the room. Shawn especially with the teacher mainly looking at him appeared angry and embarrassed at the same time.

"I will conclude with one more thing. Thank you for your attention, and your thoughts on this discussion. On the display, it will show from the Bible, Proverbs. This was written by King Solomon, thousands of years ago, when the people had the same thoughts, concerns, and tribulations as we all face today. Ron, please read this out loud to all. I'm not pushing anything, just giving you something to ponder. When done, the class will be dismissed."

The hologram disappeared and the display lit up. It paused a moment as if to give shy Ron a moment to mentally prepare. His face turned red and his voice wasn't loud, but he read it clearly.

"Prov 14:15. The simple believes every word: but the prudent consider well his steps. 16. A wise man fears and departs from evil, but the fool rages and is confident. 17. A quick-tempered man acts foolishly, and a man of wicked intentions is hated. 18. The simple inherit folly, but the prudent are crowned with knowledge."

When completed, instead of jumping up with noise the boys paused in their seats in brief quiet. Ron got up first and headed for his hidden snacks before going outside. Jeeter gave Heath a quiet knuckle touch and headed for the bathroom. Heath stood in place and stretched, as he curiously glanced down at the still sitting Shawn. Shawn's teeth were clenched, and he still looked angry and embarrassed. Heath then quickly walked away before Shawn saw him staring at him. Walking towards the gym door as they called it, he still pondered the discussion and Shawn's reaction. It seemed to Heath that Shawn was fighting an eternal battle, perhaps trying to keep an invisible wall up? As Heath walked and stretched outside, he realized he too felt his typical anger. Was he also fighting to keep up a wall? Shawn soon came outside beside him, also pausing to stretch in the now cold air. His facial expression still looked unusual to Heath.

"Everything alright fellow prisoner?" Heath ventured.

Big Shawn glanced at him with his steel-gray eyes a moment before answering.

"Sure, barf breath, what's it to you?" Grinning evilly, he continued towards his punching bag and exercise routine.

Heath smiled and shook his head. "No more cracks in that wall today," he said aloud to himself.

Jeeter had walked through the door and heard him. "Who are you talking to? You losing it bro?"

Heath grinned, "I said I was going to slap your mama and then kick your butt today as usual!"

Jeeter smirked, "You wish dork head! Up your nose with a rubber hose! Let's do it to it!"

FIVE

About a half-hour later the big helicopter from the back corner of the building took off, always away from their direction so none could see who was in it. All had paused their activity to watch it fly away and wait for its loud noise to dissipate. All of them had to dress warmer in the colder air, and all the leaves of the few trees they could see were gone. The helicopter event had occurred countless times in the past and they had always resumed playing. However, today they all strangely stayed still glancing at each other afterward. Shawn then walked towards Heath and Jeeter, and even shy Ron slowly walked towards the group keeping a safe distance behind Shawn. Ether it was the discussion today or something just snapped in all of them. It appeared they all had the same idea.

Heath spoke first, waving them first in an area hugging the outside wall. He spoke quietly. "We need to team up and break out of here. I think this fence out here is the only way."

Shawn replied quickly. "You all finally got some guts. We need a distraction and to disarm the electricity."

Jeeter responded also. "I noticed about four in the morning last week the generator stopped. I was in the bathroom. I'm guessing they fill it up with gas before breakfast".

Ron took a couple of steps closer to the group. In his shy quiet voice, he said "I noticed that too" nodding his head. About three weeks ago I think?"

Heath spoke again to the group. "Nice! Then about uhhhhh, every two weeks it seems? Early in the morning, the generator runs out of fuel until they refuel it before breakfast! The electricity will be shut off!"

Shawn now became excited. "Yes! We need to do shifts all hours of the night around then, to be ready for it. We will need heavy clothes on and the blankets to cover the top razor wire". Pointing at Ron, Shawn continued. "We will have to help Jelly Belly up the fence with a human chain to get over the top. We also will need food and water; who knows how far we are from people?" All became excited at its possibility.

Ron spoke again with shyness, but also with determination. "We will need to block the gym door, just enough". All were shocked at his truth and clever idea.

Jeeter responded admiringly. "He is right! I didn't think of the gym door! We need to drop a sock or something in the door jam to keep the auto-lock from locking completely!"

Shawn stood up and stretched while smiling as all were. "Next week than boys. Plan on supplies, shift watch, and be discrete!"

All nodded a little happier and went back to their outside fun. During the next week, Ron did his usual food hoarding, but now with the others in mind as well. Jeeter carefully studied the gym door jam area when it was open, scrutinizing how much was needed to barely block the auto-lock without being too obvious. Shawn wasn't quite as mean as he normally was and he frequently scoped out the yard area. He tried to visualize what materials they would need, and how best all could quickly get over the fence. Heath quietly talked with Jeeter in hopes of an escape. He also tried to figure out the best chance of discovery when the generator would stop. All had to be ready quickly or else they would have to wait another three weeks for another chance!

After lunch, during that week another intense discussion ensued. "Today let's talk about, Loneliness." The hologram had appeared suddenly which always made the boys jump involuntarily in their seats. Jeeter almost choked to death on the jawbreaker candy he had saved and was rolling around in his mouth. Heath thought he'd have to do the Heimlich maneuver on him that he had learned from health class in high school. Luckily, Jeeter coughed it out. The hologram having paused to watch the event with a look of concern then continued.

Its voice was magical in a way, emitting from many hidden speakers of power and clarity; few in the world were privy to it at that time period.

"Loneliness can occur with anyone of course, in different shapes and forms. It can be fleeting or eat at the pit of your stomach with pain, indefinitely. It has been said only people that you care about can cause you this pain, or else it wouldn't hurt. A person could smile at you directly, and yet feel the torment of being lonely. This can be caused by a friend, a family member, a spouse, etc. simply abandoning you, or flat out ignoring you. Sometimes they might send you a card with nothing but a scrawled signature because your time isn't worth their time, but they can now check off the box. They sent you a card and their conscious is now clear to them. A person can be lonely, even in a crowded room. We all know this to be true. However, are we conscious of it? Do we put ourselves above others, always? How do we deal with this?" Once again, all the boys became quiet, and all seemed uncomfortable. A couple of them had crossed arms, the other two had crossed legs and protectively looked down. "Heath, your thoughts?" the teacher asked while glancing at the student.

"Uhhhhhhhh... I agree with what you said. I never had that too much I guess", Heath replied hesitantly. The Hologram continued to stare at him for more. "I guess that would be horrible. Some people might even think of suicide I guess."

The hologram nodded at his answer." Yes, Heath.

Being lonely and ignored can lead to low self-esteem, self-destruction, depression, and even suicide. There are many ways people deal with this issue badly. Many put up emotional walls. Some may slowly try to eat themselves to death with food and lack of exercise. Some may get angry, at anything. They may look at anything to attack, not in hopes of destroying it, but in hopes, it will destroy themselves. Suicide by police, fighting, and dangerous jobs, all may be examples of this. Others may become uncaring. They go with the flow etc. and are so uncaring of themselves, that they might not even bother to get out of the way of a speeding truck."

Of all the discussions they had in the past, the hologram had never seen such an agonizing, painful, and emotional look on all the boys. It decided not to prod them anymore, but to leave them with a conclusion.

"Again, I'm no proclaimed expert on this subject, only someone who has more life experiences than you all. Just remember to think of others. Ignoring those around you may hurt them more you than you can possibly imagine. Remember, only the creator can see the river of time. Don't ever sub come to thoughts of suicide, in this one-time incredible existence. We can't see the future. For all you know, in a small window of time, you may have your own loving family, and perhaps a dog that puts his head on your lap every day, excited to see only you! Have faith, have faith, have faith!"

"Lastly, think about this old story. A farmer discovered his old favored mule had fallen into an old well. He figured it had broken bones, but didn't have the heart to shoot it. He decided to bury it in place without looking at it. He began to throw the dirt into the well for quite a while. When he was near completion, he looked down. He was shocked at what he saw. The mule had kept shaking off the dirt as it fell, and so the dirt kept filling in underneath, causing the mule to rise. As he continued, the mule rose to the surface, and to the joy of the farmer, it was unharmed!"

"Shawn, what is the moral of this story?"

Shawn with his arms and legs crossed now, paused and cleared his throat, and replied. "It means keep shaking the B.S off yourself, and not only you will live, but you will also rise to the top."

The hologram smiled in admiration. "Well said, Shawn!" Looking around at all of them the teacher continued. "For all of your sake and those affected by you, I pray you remember all of these discussions, and not let them dissipate in this immoral world. Always think of others and never give up. Shake off the bad, keep moving forward, and always keep the faith. I want at least a three-page well-written essay on this topic, turned in before the end of the day. Then you will be done for today." The hologram disappeared, and the boys groaned as they reached for their writing material.

As they all continued to write the essay, Jeeter stretched and yawned loudly. He cleared his throat attracting the others' attention. Jeeter smiled and used sign language moving his hands and fingers silently describing their hopeful escape. Heath started laughing and smiling at Jeeter in response.

Shawn wasn't impressed and became visibly angry. He quickly whispered loudly. "Cut it out!" he hissed while pointing in the direction of hidden cameras. Shawn then disgustingly shook his head and slapped himself in the face. "If brains were gas, they couldn't power a mini bike around the inside of a Cheerio!" he whispered to himself.

Unbeknownst to them all, a quiet discussion was occurring in the large hidden room connected to the kitchen, with its own wide double back door. Among other things, the room had two small beds and an office room of sorts that simulated a NASA control center. The room was connected to the kitchen and was all soundproof.

A taller standing person was looking down at a sitting person. The standing person was saying, "They have progressed immensely, and no doubt even with the sent letters, the families must be trying everything possible to find us. Should we finish this? We ourselves are tiring."

The sitting person paused in thought before replying. "No, not quite yet. Truth be told, I know a couple of the families aren't even hardly trying hard to find them!"

The standing person stood up taller stretching and taking a deep breath before speaking again. "You know how I feel about all this, but we have come this far, and I always keep my promises. They won't escape."

After a few more days, one morning an electric hair razor appeared on one of the desks. The high display on the wall read repeatedly, "All will cut their hair completely off in the bathroom. It will be buzzed in military basic training style. Until this is done completely, the program will fully stop, including outside privileges! Your stay here will end up even longer!

All looked at each other in disbelief and surprise. They each knew their hair was getting shaggy, but none had ever cut their own hair before, much less a butch!

Jeeter snickered, shrugged his shoulders, and grabbed the razor first. The other three followed him to the bathroom and watched laughing. Jeeter quickly completed it, following Heath, and then Ron, but only with Heath and Jeeter pushing him to the sink. As all laughed, it suddenly got quiet as the other three now stared at Shawn.

"Get out!" Shawn suddenly yelled at them. The other three walked out smirking in anticipation, and laughing at each other's appearance.

Jeeter in the classroom area pointed at Heath, yelling "Hello Charlie Brown!" Heath smiled and nodded his head. After more joking, all could hear the razor again in the bathroom.

After several minutes, Shawn yelled out, "If anybody laughs at me, they are dead meat!" When Shawn slowly came out while glaring at each of them nobody laughed. Jeeter however almost turned purple thru his black skin, as held his breath trying not to breathe and about to laugh to death! He quickly turned away from Shawn. Shawn looked a lot less menacing with his bald egg head!

Time passed, and being near the predicted shutdown of the generator, all were on high alert. There were several days of the night watch, each taking two-hour shifts before waking the next. Supplies had been gathered, and the plan was frequently discussed. Jeeter's testing of different cloth experiments being "accidentally" dropped in the doorway, cleverly prevented the auto-lock to lock completely.

While all were excited at the prospect of escaping, Heath had several nightmares. What if they failed and were caught? What would be the repercussions? Were there extreme measures of imprisonment they hadn't seen yet? If they escaped in the dark, it was sometimes very cold and stormy. Where the heck were they anyway? How many miles away from other people are they? Between night duty, and these unresolved questions on the minds of the others as well, their dispositions slowly became short.

"Yawwwwwn. Your turn to take first watch Jelly Belly! Shawn roughly said in a low voice. "Also, don't fall asleep, and don't make noise eating!" He said pointing at Ron. "Unless we missed it, this might be the night!" Shawn put his finger in his mouth and then unexpectedly shoved it into one of Ron's ears snickering....

Ron howled in disgust pulling away. "Gross! I hate wet willies!"

Shawn full out laughing evilly, then turned to head

for the bathroom. Heath and Jeeter crawled into their bunks, involuntarily smirking. Heath thought to himself aloud," I wonder who the screwball was that invented the dreaded wet willy?"

Jeeter laid back in his bunk and whispered out to Ron, who was getting out his hidden snacks for the night from under his bunk. "Bro, when you shuck him awake tonight, you better duck, tuck, and run! Believe me, I know!" Heath snickered in the dark at Jeeters usual humor, but he knew he was right. Perhaps, Shawn was right also! Maybe this was the night!

Ron survived waking Shawn up later, but barely, before passing out quickly among his empty snack papers and crumbs. Later, Shawn brutally shook and woke Jeeter up for his turn.

Jeeter shook his head awake and hissed, "OK OK! alright already!" Jeeter then silently stretched while standing up. Once awake, he sat on his bunk in the dark and began contemplating things, as he had on several shifts. Being in the dark and quiet a person is alone in their thoughts. He reflected on his life, and the many group discussions they have been having. Was he too laid back, and maybe too uncaring of himself and his future? Was he, just existing, and not living, or not trying hard? His parents were very laid back also and now were divorced. He had always been free to eat what he wanted, stay up late, and come back when he wanted. He had skipped classes and homework frequently in the past. He always had tremendous freedom and no direction. His friends were jealous and he was happy. However, he knew because of his lazy attitude he deserved the grade failure. Hence, he ended up here. He had no idea or had any plans for his future. Worse than that, was his parents' attitude a blessing, or just flat-out uncaring? Feeling bummed out, he got up and headed for the bathroom. Ron was snoring loudly suddenly and he wanted to get some space. When I get out of here, I have to get my crap together! He thought to himself, nothing in life is guaranteed. He yawned again. Thinking in the quiet dark is good sometimes he surmised. Especially when it's really quiet like now. Jeeter stopped frozen; his mouth became dry. It is quiet! The generator wasn't running! He started to freak out, but then calmed himself and remembered the plan! First, Jeeter quietly and firmly tried to push in the side door, they had slightly blocked it. If it didn't open they would have to try again another time. It opened! Very cold air flooded in from the dark early morning. He then went to the guys, quietly shaking them all awake. Everybody's hearts were pounding as they all put their shoes on in the dark, and gathered their jackets, gloves, and supplies. No night lights were shown as there was no power on. In the main room, however, all noticed the display was still showing the date and time. They all had seen this before and knew it must have battery backup. As they filed out towards the door with all their supplies, Shawn grinned in the dark and flipped the room off with his middle finger. They all felt the cold air hit them on their face as they walked into the darkness, but were glad of no rain or snow. They quickly headed to the gate facing the front.

All paused as Shawn quickly slapped the fence with the back of his gloved hand. He then took his glove off and did it again. "We are good!" he hissed quietly. Shawn quickly climbed up the tall fence, getting just below the inwardly curved top. Just like a prison, barb wire was on its end. In addition, large rolls of razor wire were along the whole top, which curved inward. He struggled to do it somewhat, as his large fingers in gloves could barely fit in the smaller mesh of the fence. Reaching the top and already sweating from effort and stress, he let go of one arm and waved for the blankets, etc. to be thrown to him. Heath grabbed a pile of sheets and blankets and threw them high as he could towards the top of Shawn.

As Shawn tried his best to throw and cover up the top of the razor-wired fence with one hand, a very loud "Bang!!!! Bang!!!" of explosions occurred next to them all inside the perimeter! The tremendous loud noise and bright light temporarily blinded them, and was deafening to them all! The surprise and power of it made Jeeter, Heath, and Ron fall to their knees and cover their ears, while also closing their eyes. Another explosion occurred, and Shawn being higher was the only one who wasn't all the way stunned. However, his eyes were blinded and his ears rang terribly. Being very strong and determined with his eyes closed, he tried pulling himself up higher over the blankets that were on top. It was a herculean effort, but being blinded, and having to crawl over the enfolding rolls of razor wire, it wasn't happening. He became entangled and exhausted by the struggle. After several minutes, a very loud voice from a speaker bellowed out. It sounded eerily similar to that of the hologram.

"The electric fence will rein-gauge in one minute! Return immediately to the inside of the building!" As they all struggled to open their eyes and with their ears still ringing, a hissing noise occurred, and white smoke could be seen in the starlight in front of the fence. To add to their confusion and fear, the loud voice repeated the warning, and actual gunfire could be heard just outside the fence! Shawn was heard cursing and thrashing at the top of the very high fence. He was stuck! "Forty-nine, forty-eight, forty-seven!" The voice was giving a count down." Heath shouted over the noise, " We gotta help Shawn!"

All three crawled and stood up to the fence bottom where Shawn was. Heath and Jeeter climbed up in a line towards Shawn. Heath used one hand to grab around Shawn's legs. Jeeter did the same to Heath. Jeeter was tall, so Ron was able to reach up and grab Jeeter's lower legs with both hands.

"Pull!" Heath yelled. As they pulled, both Heath and Jeeter had to let go and grab with both hands. They all started to slip off and lose their grip, but with some tearing of clothes, Shawn broke free, and all fell hard to the ground. As if on cue, another explosion and more gunfire occurred nearby.

The smoke was thick and smelly, and the loud voice

screamed at them to "Re-enter the building now!!" With mainly crawling in terror and leaving all supplies, the four managed to enter the building, removed the blockage, and slammed the door shut just as more gunfire occurred!

Six

All four lay on the cement floor inside the building, panting and coughing loudly. Everyone's eyes and nose were running. Their ears were ringing loudly also. All were shaking from the hard physical toll. After at least ten minutes, Shawn was the first to sit up and lean against a wall. He had some blood on his face from shallow scratches caused by the wire.

"Thanks", he said hoarsely and unashamed.

After some resting on the floor and splashing bathroom water on their faces, all stumbled to the bunks in despair and exhaustion. It became quiet, and only the returned hum of the generator outside could be heard. The soft night light in their room could be seen again. All fell asleep in total depression.

Three days passed and the hologram had still not shown itself. No food or communication was given either! They all drank from the bathroom sink, and they divided a snack found in the bedroom. Ron laid down a lot and whimpered as if dying. The others didn't feel much better. All were nauseous from lack of food and stress. Whenever they started to swear a lot and tried to smash a door or wall, instant terrible loud sirens blared out. This time, however, it lasted three times as long as before. When they tried to plug their ears and go for the speakers hidden in the ceiling, instant smoke blew out making them tired and sleepy. Even if they could stand the deterrents somehow, everything was solid cement and steel. For the first time, they all felt that could die here, by these hidden tyrants! Obviously, this had been planned out in great detail and expense. They had no freedom and their lives were completely dependent on an unseen enemy. True fear of death hit them all!

On the fourth morning, Shawn continued to weakly pace the building like a caged animal. Jeeter lay stretched out on the floor seemingly preparing for death. Heath knelled on the floor and unashamedly prayed out loud for help. Ron, with more fat on him than all the others put together, suddenly got up in the bedroom and pushed his bunk mattress off the bed. Sure enough, a crushed and months-old sweet roll was underneath. With his mouth drooling he shakily opened it and picked off a section, and then popped it lovingly in his mouth. He hesitated only a moment looking to see if anyone was looking from the larger room. They were not.... however, using more discipline than he had in his entire life he walked out to the others.

"I just found it. I already took a piece", he explained while shakily holding out in his hand. The others quickly came over to him and grabbed equal pieces. They also shakily ate it in great reverence. Afterward, Ron licked the package clean while the others sat in the chairs. They all nodded their thanks to Ron. Heath had his hands in his face while massaging his head as his stomach growled for more food. Looking up all of a sudden, he yelled out loudly.

"You win!! If you wanted us dead, you would have done it long ago! We will finish this peacefully until done! You win!!"

The others surprised at the outburst, looked hopefully towards the hologram's usual position. They were happily rewarded! The hologram appeared, and looking stern with its hands behind its back, it began speaking in its calm musical voice.

"Imagine starving to death? Imagine others controlling your life in every aspect, with no freedom, and in constant fear for the rest of your life? Before here, when you wasted opportunities and shook your hands angrily at the unfairness of the world, did you consider how lucky you are? Imagine some parents, who abandon their babies in dumpsters? Imagine the people who died for this Country or came back mentally and psychically broken? When so many in this world have no books to read, no food to eat, or no freedom to go where they please, do you then have the right to complain? Outside these walls, you were in paradise!" "You all will clean every inch of this building, and then you will receive food, and the program will resume. As you were warned, this is Indefinite Detention!"

The hologram then disappeared and they all stood up shakily to begin cleaning. Shawn for the first time cleaned hard with them, as he too was done fighting it seemed. About an hour later the kitchen area opened its cover, revealing four older peanut butter and jelly-wrapped sandwiches, and a large pitcher of cold fruit punch with cups. The heavy steel wall showed behind the food. They all devoured everything, never before enjoying food so much! When done they heard a click, and they all happily went to the side door and stepped outside! The four spread out when outside and all slowly looked up towards the sun on their face. They all breathed in the cold fresh air and enjoyed the blue sky. The fence had been cleaned of the sheets etc, and a new red-painted line three feet off the fence was on the ground, obviously indicating the restriction and boundary. After slowly walking and greatly smiling, they all spread out along the building wall and sat down in the fading winter sun.

After a good ten minutes in silence, Heath spoke his mind aloud. Jeeter was nearest to him. "They are scumbags for doing this to us, but it spoke rightly. I will never be the same again. If we ever get out of here, I will always appreciate my freedom, my family, and a lot more!"

Jeeter leaned his head back to the wall, facing the blue

sky he closed his eyes and breathed in deeply the fresh air. "Ditto brother, ditto."

The routine of bookwork, tests, rewrites of papers, and discussions continued the next day. Shawn was the slowest but again was frequently aided by Ron who was always jumpy around him. Perhaps for additional punishment, deserts were not given out anymore, and the outdoor area opened less. Occasionally, Tab Cola was given out as an option. Even though it was diet, at least it was a variety of water.

The result of this was they seemed less hyper, and they had more study time. They all instinctively felt they were over the hump, in whatever experiment this was. They voiced that opinion together in private.

That night in their bunks, Jeeter began his usual joking. Facing Heath in the dark, he asked "How many letters are there in the alphabet?

Heath laying on his back replied quickly, "26 of course"

Jeeter smiled in anticipation, "Nope, it's 22, cuz E.T went home and somebody shot J.R ! Whaaaa haaaaaa!!!" Heath chuckled out loud with him, and Ron rolled his eyes in the dark.

Shawn growled in the dark," Why don't you guys talk about something interesting, like babes, for instance?

"Jeeter quickly piped up " Shooooot, all the ladies love me, they think I'm funny!"

Shawn fired back," Maybe so, but did you ever get lucky?" Everybody was silent..... Shawn sat up quickly in

the dark. "Do you mean to tell me all of you are virgins?!"
More silence.... "Hahahaha, what a bunch of losers!"

Heath's temper kicked in, "OK big shot, tell us your tales of B.S with the babes!"

Shawn silently debated with himself if he should pound Heath for that, but instead, after a pause, he laid back down and snickered out loud. "OK, I'll throw you guys a bone. You guys need all the help you can get. Heck, Ron over there is probably spanking his monkey!"

Heath and Jeeter couldn't help a snicker, and Ron could be heard angrily turning over on his side.

"Don't sweat it jelly belly, I'm sure there is a nerd out there for you somewhere." Shawn continued. "Alright, step one! Find a babe that seems to like you and wants to talk. Someone you like also of course. Take her out somewhere etc. Step two, get her alone and start petting her, kissing her, squeezing her, etc. Keep in mind their engine takes longer than ours, you can't expect to put your drill bit in the hole right away!"

In the dark Heath and Jeeter were smirking, but were riveted at what he was saying. Even Ron could be heard quietly turning back over to hear better.

"Step three! Make sure she is not on the rag, and that you have your rubber glove on! Unless of course, you want to have a little rug rat. Lastly, put your pole in her hole, go in and out, and then pop goes the weasel!"

Jeeter and Heath started clapping in the dark chuckling

Jeeter shouted out, "That's what I'm talking about! We need to get out of here!"

Heath laughed, "Yea, we can all walk out on three legs!" Even Shawn snickered at that in the dark also. Little by little they all stopped laughing and began to settle down.

As it got quiet, Ron's whisper towards Heath could be heard, "What is a rag, a rubber glove, and three legs mean?"

A tidal wave of laughter from the other three began again. It was several minutes before Heath got his breath back and explained it to him.

Jeeter laying on his back was thoughtful. His bunk was unusual as it was long enough for his 6'3 tall skinny frame. He was silently glad he wasn't the only virgin in the room. He thought of his divorced parents. Physical attraction is great of course, but with his parents, there was a lack of caring and respect. "Hmmm," he thought out loud unknowingly, "Yes, caring and respect, maybe things would have been different" he mused softly. He thought of his younger brother and himself dealing with the yelling, crying, and accusations of his parents against each other. During birthdays and holidays, they dealt with the parents arguing about sharing the kids. He thought of all the arguments during their marriage, and then the weirdness of seeing his parents with other partners after the breakup. Divorce is horrible for all. Perhaps, some people should not have gotten together in the first place.... Even in the closeness of sleep, the other three heard Jeeter's self-remarks in the dark. They heard the quiet" yes, caring and respect, maybe things would have been different". They all knew what he was referring to. Perhaps because he was one of them, his words were burned in their young minds.

In the hidden room beside the kitchen, two others laid in the late dark of the night also. One sleeping, and one awake, smiling while listening to the teenagers' conversation. The volume from the speakers/headphones in the control room was very low. There were listening devices everywhere, in the building and outside area. There were also small high-tech video cameras in the kitchen, outside play area, and the far surrounding area of the building. No cameras were in the bathroom or bedroom for privacy. Listening to the teenager's conversation got the awake person thinking and reflecting on memories and innocence.

If I could go back in time... (the awake person thought) Would I start as a young child, teenager, or middle age and later, etc.? A young child is usually care-free, innocent, and worry-free, having a lot of fun and being cared for. However, the child is at the mercy of all, and subject to any manipulation. A teenager is more developed and self-aware but is still trying to figure himself or herself out, with the hopes and worries of the future, intimacy with the opposite sex, and trying to fulfill all societies' expectations. In middle age hopefully, the obstacles of school, learning about the world, having a career and family, etc. are mostly accomplished.

Listening to the teenagers made the person think; at that age dreams and experiences are all new and exciting. All can be striven for. Time should never be wasted, or unappreciated. The person rolled over in bed and thought, better hit the hay. Breakfast would have to be prepared in the morning and another day of challenges would begin!

Heath, Ron, Jeeter, and Shawn sat lazily in their chairs. They had done their bookwork and now just finished lunch. They were all hoping for an early day, as this was technically Friday for them. Some days went by like molasses and others having fiery discussions flew by. Sometimes they were cut loose early for whatever reason, and like a bear getting lucky once with a trash can of food, the hope and possibility of it happening again was always a motivator. The hologram appeared after bookwork, lunch, and break as usual.

"Let's talk about real life! Do people in real life have perfect lives? As on TV, do good people always win in the end? Do all people have shaven or clean faces, sometimes covered in makeup? Do all have perfect bodies, perfect speech, etc., etc.? Don't people in real life make mistakes, and sometimes trip over their own feet? Should people copy each other and try to be like those perfect fake people on TV, in movies, or Magazines? Aren't we all different, and bring something to the table, in different ways? Don't we all have a right to be here? Jeeter, you start!"

"Heeeekkkkck! I'm perfect. I'm gorgeous and cool!

People on TV wished they could be like me!" Jetter replied smiling. Everybody laughed.

"Do you make mistakes Jeeter?" asked the hologram.

"Ahhhhhh....on very rare occasions.....haha....Yes, I make mistakes of course" Jetter replied.

"Do you have something of use or value, or ability, or some type of goodness to aid in humankind?" asked the hologram.

"Sheeeze man, this deal is getting deep! Well, uhhhh-hh.... besides my awesome coolness and humor, I like to think I'd be a good song lyrics writer and basketball player one day!"

The hologram nodded its head. "Do you think you'll have some failures or an occasional locked door in that endeavor? Will you make mistakes and give up early trying that profession?" asked the hologram.

Jeeter fired back, "Nooo, I'm no quitter! Singers or basketball teams would be lucky to have someone like me!"

Heath rolled his eyes and smiled; he admired his friend's new determination, especially as he himself was shy and sometimes doubtful of himself.

"Thank you Jeeter,", said the hologram smiling. "At the minimum Jeeter, your easy-going and humorous atti-tude relaxes people and makes them smile in the most stressful of times. "Mr. Ron! How about you sir? Do you make mistakes in life? Do you have value and contribute to society?" asked the hologram.

As usual, Ron was red-faced and shy, and looking

down as always he shrugged his shoulders. He patiently and agonizingly waited for the frequent interrogation to pass by him. The hologram, however, did not yield this time but instead kept its gaze on him. As the other boys leaned back with their hands behind their back preparing for a possible snooze opportunity, the hologram continued its interrogation relentlessly.

"You're going to have to answer this time my friend. No more skipping over. Remember, no answer is wrong, this is just a discussion among friends. Do you make mistakes like all of us?" asked the hologram, who was leaning more forward than normal towards Ron.

Shawn leaned forward and looked closer at the hologram, wondering if more of its cleavage would be seen. Heath and Jeeter noticed, and followed suit smirking. All three leaned back at the same time, discovering that doesn't work on holograms.

"Yes, I make mistakes" Ron replied in a quiet voice, still looking down bashfully.

"Also, do you have any value? Do you have abilities, acts of kindness, skills, etc.. that could benefit society?" asked the hologram. A long uncomfortable pause ensued, making the other three boys close their eyes in rest and boredom.

Ron glanced sideways at the other boys briefly, his face becoming redder. In a small voice looking down, Ron replied, "I don't know...I guess. People don't ask my opinion, they never have." A further pause, then Ron unexpectedly stood up and raised his voice, red-faced and loud. "I get seated in front of the TV at home and I get fed! Daily! That's it! No opinion asked, no requests, no nothing! That's it! That's me!" Ron shouted turning away and hiding his tears, with his body shaking, hands clenching." I hate this questioning; you have no right! I hate this place; you all sicken me!" Ron stomped away and headed towards the bathroom slamming the door shut.

The never before seen outburst of Ron surprised and shocked the others to quiet. "Class dismissed", the hologram said suddenly before disappearing. The side door to the outside was heard unlocking.

After a moment Jeeter broke the silence, "Let's do some b-ball bro!" as he jumped up and headed for the outside door smiling. Heath, while sympathetic to Ron, smiled also and was only half a step behind his friend, quickly forgetting the tension that had been in the room. Soon music and laughing were heard from outside, along with the bouncing of a basketball.

Shawn continued to sit in his chair, leaning back and thoughtful. Being alone so much and of course, drying out from drugs had made him reflect a lot. Unbeknown to the others still, Shawn's mother had died from cancer when he was young. After which his father had done the classic drinking too much, and had many girlfriends over time. He was pretty much neglected, except for the yelling and belt beating by his father when he misbehaved. The belt never seemed to care where it hit on his young body. The city streets became his home. Shawn became tough and self-reliant, with many mental walls up, and he developed a chip on his shoulder. He enjoyed mechanics and gym class in High School, but the drugs in his last year slowed him down, hence his last school year failure, as the others now with him. Truth be told, for a while, he didn't care if he lived or died. At this moment, however, a mental wall had fallen, a feeling he had not experienced in a long time... perhaps since his mother was living.

Ron was still in the bathroom, punching his own hands and angry with himself and the world. He missed home badly of sorts. An empty void filled his gut as he stared at himself in the mirror; his soft fat body engulfing the mirror's space. As an only child he initially received a lot of attention from his parents, but then things changed. They became more and more engrossed with their ever-demanding careers. Even at a young age, Ron was left alone a lot with nothing but easily accessible junk food and a TV for a babysitter. No guidance or direction was given to him, just a hi and bye each day.

A loud knock came at the door making Ron jump. "Alright, quit playing with yourself and come on out!" Shawn said smiling from the other side.

"I'm not playing with myself; I was hitting my hand in anger!" Ron yelled back from inside the bathroom.

"Whatever you say, dork, just come on out, you and I are going to box!" said Shawn with an evil grin. Ron was suddenly terrified; he knew he had to come out sooner or later. A quiet long pause occurred.

"What? Wha wha why?" he quivered. "I did nothing to you!" Ron replied in a meek and still quivering voice.

Shawn lowered his voice, "Don't have a cow dude! Geeeze I'm not going to hurt you, I'm just going to show you some moves. I won't hurt you I promise! Unless of course you tick me off and don't come out of there!" Shawn added. It took more banging on the door, but finally, it opened.

"I don't know how to box," Ron said meekly looking down ashamed.

"Look dork head, sorry, I mean Ron. It's no big deal! We will just move around the ring. You can just try to hit me" Shawn said lowering his voice.

Ron was suspicious, terrified, and shocked. Shawn had said the word "sorry!" "OK, I'll try," Ron said stammering."

Shawn smiled," Let's do it to it!"

It was a beautiful afternoon, with a cool breeze and fresh mountain air. Heath and Jeeter had worked up a sweat playing. Both were ragging each other with insults as they played one on one basketball. It was the one thing in this" school prison" that made it tolerable, being able to have fun and vent out their anxiety.

"Bitchin"! Jeeter yelled as he easily jumped up with his tall body and slammed a dunk in.

"Nice one" Heath grudgingly said giving his friend credit. Heath now having the ball faced the net with Jeeter ready to block. Heath faked a couple of starts. "Psych!" he said before bouncing the ball between Jeeter's tall legs and completing an unchallenged layup. "Ha! What happened to your bro!" Heath said smiling and bouncing the ball. He looked at Jeeter who was now staring with his jaw open towards the school's side entrance

"You better call an ambulance!" Jeeter mumbled, as now both of them stared unbelieving at the huge Shawn and short fat Ron, walking towards the boxing ring entrance. Both were wearing boxing gloves!! "This is serious #$!%" Jeeter whispered

"Totally!" Heath replied in wonder....

As the weeks continued, the surreal relationship between Shawn and Ron continued. Ron aided Shawn with bookwork with less fear it seemed, and Ron began to lose weight. They all noticed also, that Ron wheezed a lot less when walking or doing the required cleaning and daily chores. When Shawn and Ron exercised together, Shawn pushed him hard like a drill sergeant. Heath and Jeeter would stop and stare in wonder! It was beyond belief!!

"Hit it like you mean it, sissy boy!" Shawn could be heard yelling at Ron who was sweating and trying to hit the heavy bag with Shawn holding it from behind.

Ron suddenly stopped and yelled back at him. "Stop calling me sissy boy! I never boxed before! I never did anything before! Also, you suck at math!" Ron hollered while standing still and huffing and puffing, sweat pouring off him even though it was cool outside.

Heath and Jeeter froze, both tensed up, ready to run

and defend Ron in a sure beating from Shawn. Jeeter held the basketball tight, thinking he may have to drill it at Shawn. Both stared in awe and disbelief when it didn't happen! At Ron's outburst and personal insult, big Shawn did pause, but only for a moment. He then laughed! "OK, OK", he said laughing and shaking his head. " Just keep hitting the bag!"

Heath and Jeeter, frozen and standing with their mouths still wide open, slowly turned and stared at each other.

"Pigs do fly!" Jeeter whispered aloud in astonishment.

Heath nodded his blonde head up and down in agreement and whispered back. "Ron is standing up for himself, and with Shawn of all people! I accidentally swallowed my gum! I'm dead serious!"

Jeeter stood up with a relaxed smile now that there apparently wasn't a crisis. "Don't worry, it probably will only bounce around for seven years, and only sticks to stuff once in a while!" When you crap, you will probably blow a bubble!"

SEVEN

The incredibly realistic life-size female hologram faced the four male teenagers' students/captives, intently. They have been here a year now learning, fighting with each other, and even on occasion secretly crying. School subjects were increasingly intense and they had discussions on many topics. Only the promise of release, upon all of them completing the objectives, has sustained them. Having been through it all in close quarters with each other they had formed a type of brotherhood, all though none would have admitted it. The students were excited and were attentively listening and squirming in the individual comfortable desks which were bolted to the ground. They had been getting hints that this would be the day they would be freed and returned home!

"If you could wish one wish for yourself, a personal ability only, what would it be?" The teaching hologram's voice was sharp with clarity throughout the large so-called classroom. Its female blue eyes showing more intensity than normal. Its stance was standing with arms folded behind its back and standing higher than the four of them. The required responses started from whomever the hologram looked at, so Heath answered as it stared with a concentration on him alone.

Heath was anxious to be done." I guess I'd like to be able to sing," he said. Normally the others would snicker and make remarks, but like Heath, they were anxious to play the game and hopefully go home!!

"Why? she questioned. "Be honest."

He replied, "I don't know. I guess it would be cool to make people cheer for you, with everyone having fun. I can't sing, I stink at it."

The teacher responded, "Sooooooo.... you want to do something you enjoy, and that would also make other people happy?"

"Yeah, I guess so" Heath voiced.

The teacher then asked." If everyone on Earth could sing the same vocally, with all only having that one same ability, would that be better than all people having different abilities?"

"Hmmm, no, of course not," Heath responded quickly.

"Can others sing to the world in their way, using their own ability, doing things they enjoy, and that makes other people happy? Does not a good leader, a nurse, a teacher, policeman, engineer, writer, mechanic, etc., or someone who picks up trash that is not his or hers, or opens a door for someone with a smile, instead of ignoring them. Is that not all, singing to the world?... Doing something you enjoy, that puts smiles on people's faces, and improves their lives? Listen to me carefully this one last time all of you!"

All the students quickly sat up ramrod straight with hearts pounding out of their chests, at the words, "One last time!!!!!!!!!" The Hologram intensified in brightness as if all had led to this moment.

"Make sure your will and effort, are to have self-control, perseverance, and mutual affection for others. Avoid corruption, for it will make you ineffective and unproductive." She closed both her hands and lifted each one high on each side of her." Pretend each hand holds a seed, signifying potential and growth, an individual. None of you are the same. All fingerprints are unique as you are, past, present, and future. Even identical twins have different fingerprints. There will never be another you, in all time." She opened one hand. "You can drop your seed, rot in drugs, self-pity, unforgiving, laziness, anger, and despair. Wasting it forever, destroyed." Or, she paused, carefully laying her other hand down and seemingly placing the seed on the ground, patting it with a hand from above. "You can plant the seed, be kind and patient with yourself, be satisfied with yourself, and not by sole judgment of others. The tree will slowly grow with deep roots in the ground, able to withstand any storm. It will provide oxygen, fruit, shade, shelter, bring beauty to itself and others... it will sing... to the world!"

The students sat up bright-eyed as if a light of thought had burned away a black curtain of darkness in their minds. The hologram disappeared, and the sound of an automatic lock came from behind them. A steel door that had been locked and that had imprisoned them for more than a year was finally opened! Bright sunshine poured in, and they ran to it laughing, light in heart, eyes bright, and ready to go home!

The same bus that had brought them there a year ago was parked in the front. No driver was seen, it was empty. A man in his fifties wearing an oxygen mask and sitting in a wheelchair was near its opened door. A cap was on his bald head. He lifted his right hand and weakly waved at the four suspicious teenagers, who were slowly approaching with great caution. As they approached closer, the four noticed he had four large red envelopes in his lap. He looked frail as if he could die at any moment. A nurse about fifty years old was holding the handles of the wheelchair. She smiled and looked down as if embarrassed and worried. The wheeled chairman tried to raise his weak shaky voice as best he could, but it was low in strength.

"Have no fear. A map of where you are and how to get home is on the bus. Arrangements have been made for you all at the nearest bus station. There is food and a CB radio in there if you need to call for help. There are several private gates down the mountain; the map has the gate codes." He took a moment to pause and slowly breathe in through an oxygen mask. He lifted an envelope and handed one to Shawn the closest, and then one to each of the others. "This contains some answers, cash, and a check in your name. Follow the instructions carefully to get it cashed. Drive carefully, and know this will never happen again. May God be with you all." He weakly raised his hand in goodbye. As the nurse started to turn him away, the wheeled chairman's eyes lingered on Heath. A side view revealed he was crying many tears.

All four carefully looked around in astonishment and suspicion... frozen in time.

Finally, after several moments of silence, Jeeter yelled "Let's make like a tree and leave!" Shawn went in first getting into the driver's seat. Jeeter and Ron showing no objection went in also and found seats in the back. As the bus started up, Heath lingered at the bus door entrance, watching the nurse push the frail man away. He also noticed the older distinguished bus driver that brought them here, was exiting the school entrance and quickly walking towards the wheel-chaired man. He could also hear a helicopter in the distance.

"Come on Heath, help me with this map as I drive the hell out of here! "shouted Shawn with one hand on the door closer handle. Heath nodded his head and started up, but only to pause again blocking the door from closing. Heath again looked toward the school, all three older adults going quickly into the entrance, and the helicopter was getting louder and visible in the sky.

Heath suddenly turned to look towards Shawn's anxious face. "You guys go! Don't worry about me! I'll see you again!" Heath looked towards the back at the other two, "You guys go without me!" Heath then turned away and ran towards the entrance of the school.

"Wait!", yelled Jeeter now standing watching Heath run away. The bus suddenly lurched forward turning away hard towards the road and with the door closing. Jeeter fell backward, while Ron pressed his face against the window watching in amazement.

Shawn was done with all this! "Jeeter" he yelled," I need help with the map!"

Heath ran hard, his heart was in his throat, fighting every instinct to head back to the bus. A quick glance behind him showed it was too late anyway, the bus was quickly speeding away. As he entered the school he saw it to be empty. The helicopter sound indicated it was landing in the basketball area in the back. He quickly ran through the side entrance. The helicopter landed and the three adults were waiting nearby, heads down low. As Heath approached them the nurse noticed him first.

"Look!" She cried out pointing at him with her finger.

The bus driver turned and calmly walked towards Heath with a stern face. "Why are you still here son? You are free to go home.!" He had to yell over the noise. "

"I want answers!!" Heath yelled, anger and fear flooding him.

The elder man paused frowning... then nodded his

head. He turned towards the helicopter waving his arms and slashing his throat with his palm, indicating for it to shut down. When the helicopter shut down, all adults and Heath stood in a circle outside. "We don't have much time Heath, but now it's unavoidable."

Heath asked, "Who are you? Really?"

The tall distinguished man paused a second and replied. "In truth, I'm all four of you together... Like all of us, I've had the best teacher in the universe, he said pointing his finger to the sky and smiling. "It's just that I've lived longer."

The bus driver turned away, lightly patting the wheel-chaired man on the shoulder as he walked away. The nurse followed him, leaving the wheel-chaired man and Heath alone in semi-privacy. Heath took a breath and tried to calm himself before asking "Who are you? Why all of this?" lifting both his arms in the air.

The chaired man looking even more pale and weak looked up. "I made many mistakes in my life, and wanted to make amends before it was too late..."He looked down and mumbled sadly, "I am your Dad Heath" A stunned silence followed. "I was a drunk and angry man, driving your mother away. I did some bad things, but many years later I got lucky by winning the lottery. After more drinking and drugs, wasting my life and a lot of money, the mentor saved me......from myself. I learned all life is precious, even mine."

"My dad...? No way!" Heath yelled, he died before I was born!"

The chaired man gently shook his head. "No. Your mother will tell you it is true, although she probably thinks I'm truly dead by now."

Heath looked hard into the chaired man's eyes, both faces flushed and emotional. Heath knew those eyes and his facial features. He suddenly knew this to be true! After a long pause and heavy breathing, tears welled in Heath's eyes. He clenched his fists in anger...." You had no right! Why? Why? Why?" he yelled loudly with his voice cracking. "Tell me!" Heath gripped the wheelchair and shook it hard.

The nurse and the bus driver suddenly ran back towards him, "Stop! they yelled. Heath stopped and stepped back. The nurse came back and helped put the oxygen mask back on.

After several moments the chaired man weakly continued. "My good friend and mentor, who was yours as well as the hologram, saved me from my ways" pointing towards the bus driver. "I did all this, with his help, although he was against it."

Heath was beyond words. He stared incredulous, noticing the nurse seemed emotionally attached to the chaired man, his father.

"Truth is Heath, I followed your life but knew in my past state I would never be accepted. I was barely surviving myself until recent years. I knew of your troubles, and wanted to help before I died.... "

"You're dying?" Heath stammered with more emotion.

"Yes, of terminal cancer. Too much smoking/drinking and abusing my body I imagine. I wanted to see and know you, to help educate you, and leave you and your friends' money, to do good in the world" His father with tears running down his face slumped forward.

"We have to go!" yelled the mentor suddenly, making hand movements to the helicopter to start back up.

As the adults started to turn and the helicopter started up, Heath grabbed the chair, "Wait, we can face this together!" His father was still slumped over with no response.

The bus driver/ mentor/teacher firmly pushed Heath back. "Please, go home Heath. Let him die in peace. Not in pain, and not in jail!" They quickly turned and went into the helicopter, as Heath stepped back in shock and disbelief. The helicopter then slowly rose in the air, and he could see his father's pale face pressed against the window, waving goodbye... Heath stood like a statue, watching the helicopter fade away into the blue sky with tears running down his face.

"Come on dweeb, let's go home!" Recognizing Shawn's now rare emotional voice, Heath turned around to see his returned friends behind him! Yes, friends in the plural. All three were astonished and emotional as he was.

As they all walked away together, Jeeter stated." You won't believe how much these freaking checks are! ... Oh well... no butts, no guts, no coconuts!" They all laughed in emotional relief... now brothers forever... ready to improve themselves... and the world.

Extra Credit- Heath

"Life. We begin, we end... Why—does it matter? How insignificant we are, how big we think ourselves. Some live! Some want! Some Suffer! It's all perceived so differently.

The ladder never ends, always climbing, always hoping, never satisfied, until oblivion we fall. What then, will we change, how?

So we go, tall in the saddle, on our stomachs, in the dark, with our mask... but we go, and go, blazing our path, until the end....?"

Extra Credit - Shawn

"I came, I saw, I changed the channel."
(Yes, you dip wads that did this to us, you can read between the lines...!")

EXTRA CREDIT- JEETER

"Who cares. No skin off my nose! Ha-ha, that's the old me... Check this out. I pat myself on the back, I'm freaking awesome!" What do you do, when you see a little bee? You tickle his belly, and he says hee hee! Then he runs to find a tree, and goes wee wee! He then slaps his knee, saying hee hee!

EXTRA CREDIT- RON

"The sun will rise tomorrow; I see that now...
Me, myself and I, that's who controls my
destiny now...!"

Teacher's last advice

"We are not puppets. We all have been given free will. The choices you make are your own. We all make mistakes, but we can be forgiven and change anytime we choose. Like the ripples in a pond from a thrown rock, our actions affect ourselves and many others, for a long time afterward... Enjoy the little things in life, and always be yourself. You were made special, by the good Lord above!"

AFTERWORD

Over five years had passed. After the reunions, the police investigations, the tears, and the interviews, all four of them became world news and kind of celebrities for a time. The public wanted to hear their incredible story. The police eventually located the "Indefinite Detention" location after a time with the map, but everything was completely gone, nothing but flattened earth was left. A property check indicated a large amount of the remote farmland in North Carolina had been purchased by an unknown corporation that did not seem to exist. The land then a year later had been secretly donated to that County for troubled youth activities, boy scouts, young military cadets, etc.....

All four teenagers graduated high school with flying colors. Later, each of them attended various colleges and universities. They used the money given to them for tuition, and to help their families.

Incredibly, Shawn and Ron later hooked up and opened a large fitness facility, which later turned into a chain. Ron and his wife did the finance work, and of course Shawn and his girlfriend did the fitness work and instruction. They routinely gave inexpensive rates to low-income teenagers, as well as yearly scholarship money to promising youths. They became friends for life.

Jeeter and Heath called each other frequently, and all four of the now-grown men got together every year. Jeeter obtained a BA degree and became a basketball coach at a large high school in his hometown. He frequently substituted for teachers and encouraged students to work hard, play hard, and be cool like he was. He was beloved by all the students. They loved to hear his made-up songs and jokes.

Heath one sunny afternoon in Florida was walking out of a university en route to his car to meet his wife for lunch. He was thinking of being a teacher of American History, including its Christian background and laws. Currently, he was close to his master's degree, and also had some real estate investments with his wife. While approaching the parking lot a very large new black limo slowly pulled up in front of him blocking his path. Heath immediately backed up and became alert. He was strong, always staying athletic, and prepared himself for any necessary action.

The limo's front passenger door opened and a small lawyer-looking person in a suit stepped out smiling. "Heath, I presume, he said?"

"Who is asking? Heath replied suspiciously.

"Heath, forgive me for coming straight to the point. Your real dad passed away, soon after you had last seen him five years ago. Recently also, your mentor/teacher has also passed away." He paused to let Heath digest that before continuing." A multi-million-dollar company that they both had majority stock in is now yours. You can sell it, change its course, control it, anything you want! I have all the papers for you to sign at the office. Additionally, your dad left you a message." He opened the back door of the limo, "Just sit inside, push that large white button, and we will drive to my office."

The lawyer also handed Heath a piece of paper. The paper had a picture of the smiling mentor/teacher. On the bottom was written, "Don't worry Heath, Indefinite Detention is over. My best wishes to you! Teacher"

Heath then scanned around cautiously. He looked carefully at the lawyer, the older driver in the limo, and again at the paper. "OK, but first we need to meet my wife Becky at the restaurant."

The lawyer smiled and opened the passenger door wider for him. " Of course, sir."

Heath got into the limo and it began moving right away. The limo was very fancy and smelled new. Heath looked around slowly again and finally pushed the button with reservations. A hologram of his younger-looking father suddenly appeared sitting next to him! Heath pushed back hard being totally shocked and startled. The hologram was very vivid in detail, and perfect speakers echoed its voice. It was the voice of his dad.

"Hello, Heath my son". It looked directly at him, seemingly tracking his face, and looked incredibly real... It continued, "Unlike your teacher's hologram, this one is pre-programmed. I am now deceased, but the company is not. With the mentor's help, his resources, and some left-over money I had to invest, I was blessed by becoming a part of it. It has some truly genius people. We do ahead of its time technology, for the benefit of the Country's defense, for wounded soldiers, for education, and for world charity, etc. Its mission is for the good of mankind, not evil or greed. We also assist new American-made companies, that make products of lasting quality and are environmentally friendly. It's in your hands now." The hologram swallowed hard. "I am very proud of you Heath. It is time for you... to sing to the whole world!" See you on the other side son!" It smiled, and slowly faded away.

Heath stared at the now-empty seat beside him, totally choked up and suddenly feeling empty. After a full minute, he leaned back and stared out of the moving limo's window. All was silent in the soundproof back seat. Buildings, cars, and trees flashed by as he stared out. He took a deep breath and reflected on his friends, who were more like brothers now. He himself had combined all their many attributes he thought, just as the mentor had been. Like Ron, Jeeter, and Shawn combined, he now had controlled his old anger. They all had developed a sprinkle of shyness, caution, humor, intelligence, caring, calmness, maturity, and courage. He was ready! He sat upright and grinned with confidence, thinking of the lion in Shawn. "Watch out World, here we come. Here we come!

SOURCES

New King James Holy Bible: Regarding Proverbs and Creation.

Personal Life Experiences.

Dr. Kent Hovind's Youtube channel: Regarding Creation

Internet Surfing: Regarding Plato and Identical Twins, by John Hughes

About the Author

I was born in California in 1965. My Dad then moved our family of five to the Vermont mountains in 1970, where he had been born. My Dad became a RN supervisor, and was a believer in the belt for punishment. Being the oldest I deserved it often for being a tease to my sister Jeannie and brother Kevin. My mom, a quiet shy christian, had to hide in a room crying so not to watch the punishment. Vermont wages were low so my dad worked two jobs. We ate things like powdered milk and our garden food. We raised chickens, rabbits, turkeys and pigs for meat. Also, in school my siblings and I ate the low income free lunches at school.

At thirteen years old my parents divorced. Later, my mom remarried a hard working dairy farmer and had two more boys, my half brothers. My step dad also had two boys from a previous marriage. So we had a total of nine people, one bathroom, and lived in a 200 year old farm house. We frequently walked down the mountain in the snow to get to the school bus.

In 1983 I graduated High School, and as I had no car or college money I enlisted in the U.S Army for three years as a Military Policeman. I was stationed in Germany and then Alabama. During which among other things, I received a rare German silver marksmanship award with special orders to be able to wear it on my dress uniform. In basic training, I was also the only one in the company who tested 40 out of 40 with the M16 rifle. On the way to walk up to receive the plaque reward, an African American drill sergeant stepped out of formation to give me a high five. As I was 18, and fresh off a remote small town farm, he had to show me what that was. I was embarrassed at my ignorance.

After an honourable discharge I drove to Florida, everything I owned was in my car. I had a total of $800.00 in cash. I used my Army collage fund to obtain an AA degree, and then took some criminal justice classes at UCF. During this time, I worked various part time jobs. My brother Kevin moved to Florida also, and we shared expenses. We ate a lot of cheap food and had cardboard boxes for furniture. Later in life, Kevin wrote the first book in the family titled "That's what Brothers are For."

In 1989, I entered and graduated from the State of Florida Marine Patrol Academy as a State Law Enforcement Officer. I also became a born again Christian soon after. We all sin everyday, but I know where I'm going after death. Later, it changed to the Florida Fish and Wildlife Commission. Eventually, I became a Field Training Officer and obtained several plaques and awards in my career. One of which was the Officer of the year award in the year 2000. After 26 years as a State Officer, I retired after having shoulder surgery. I married my better half 30 years ago. My wife, (an RN) is the smartest woman I know. We have two awesome children. Our son is a HVAC Tech and involved in church with his wife and kids. Our daughter is a Surgical/ICU RN and recently engaged to her love—The Lord has surely blessed me in so many ways!